Rare Bird Alert

R.H. PEAKE

Rare Bird Alert
This book is written to provide information and motivation to readers. Its purpose is not to render any type of psychological, legal, or professional advice of any kind. The content is the sole opinion and expression of the author, and not necessarily that of the publisher.

Printed in the United States of America.

ISBN 978-1-953150-18-9 (Paperback)
ISBN 978-1-953150-19-6 (Digital)

Lettra Press books may be ordered through booksellers or by contacting:

Lettra Press LLC
30 N Gould St. Suite 4753
Sheridan, WY 82801, USA
1 307-200-3414 | info@lettrapress.com
www.lettrapress.com

Rare Bird Alert
by Richard H. Peake
Lettra Press

book review by Joel Samberg
US REVIEW OF BOOKS

*"The soft strains of Mozart's Clarinet Concerto in A Major comple-
mented Georgina's voice with what Bob thought was a sexy background."*

With a curious cast of characters, a travelogue of colorful
locales, and a query into why unusual characters do what they
do in picturesque places, this book is about human reactions
to various non-human and decidedly inhuman things. The
non-human things include birds and natural settings, while
the inhuman things include rape and murder. From Australia
to Galveston to a South Pacific island, from lonely people to
nosy people to bad people, from sparrows to orioles to kookaburras, this book is a unique expedition into bird-watching
and crime, told in a literary style that often appears casual,
here and there caustic, perhaps even semi-satirical. The
result is a twenty-four chapter excursion into fiction that is
sometimes too strange to be believed but also too observant
not to have some truth behind it.

While the narrative flow is a bit unusual, the book makes up
for it in a tale as unique as they come. The storytelling leaves
the impression that this singular effort was written in something akin to a literary monotone. The characters are not
exceedingly easy to care about, but the promise is there, beginning with the work's intriguing title. This puts the reader in a
curious mood, making one instantly wonder if this work will

duplicate the tone of a whimsical movie like *The Big Year,* the 2011 film about bird enthusiasts who try to outdo each other, or if it will be closer to Steve Martin's own *Rare Bird Alert,* in which the comedian plays the banjo and provides lyrics and music lessons. **Peake's novel is unlike either one. Instead, it is distinctive in its own right, a distinction that comes from its unusual and sprawling storyline.**

Books By R.H. Peake

From Papaw to Print: A History of Appalachian Literature,
Mapplelodge Publication,1990

Wings Across
Vision Books,1992

Birds of Virginia Cumberlands
Mapplelodge Publication,2001

Soon to be available:

LETTRA PRESS publication

Jaykyll's Joust
Moon's BLACK GOLD
Beauty'S No Biscuit
Love and Death on Safari

Chapter One

Margaret Smith stood in line at busy Bush International Airport in Houston waiting to board a flight for Australia. Watching the passing parade as she walked slowly with her boarding group, she was glad she had only one change of planes on her way to down under. A widow, she was looking forward to her trip to the land of her birth. Over a year of widowhood had passed, and she felt a need for more than the garden club and membership in Birds & Floats to occupy her time and push away the loneliness. Her marriage to Hank had been very happy, though he had been twenty years older. She missed him.

Her life like a vacant landscape without him, she had recently begun a list of the bird species she had identified and was looking forward to expanding this list with many strange birds in Australia.

She enjoyed the odors from the food shop and the noise of the crowd. Loneliness is terrible, Margaret had discovered. Hank was the only man she'd known in a physical way, though she had had some experience with women, before her marriage, when she was sixteen. Hank had left her very well off, but aching for his humor, companionship, and knowledge of how to arouse her passion. She found going to bed without him very difficult, and she regretted that she and

Hank had delayed so long in having children because they, especially Hank, were enjoying freedom to take trips, play golf and watch sports on television. Hank had put aside some of his sperm to assure her she could have a baby by him if he died. She was comforted by the thought of it. She hoped to use it, but, worried about raising a child alone, thought she'd wait awhile.

Though she had just celebrated her twenty-ninth birthday, she had stayed active and watched her diet. Looking at herself as she inspected her mirror image in the airport glass, Margaret approved of what she saw, naturally blond hair, an excellent figure and a face that retained her youthful beauty. She had decided, after looking at books and brochures about her native land, a birding tour of Australia would be a wonderful way to occupy her time, make new friends, and build a long bird list, while having a great adventure. She was just a beginner at watching birds but had already been challenged by her friends at Birds & Floats to build what they called a life list. She had found watching beautiful birds complemented her love of colorful flowers and human companionship. For her the social aspects of bird watching were as rewarding as seeing and listing the birds.

⁚ ⁚ ⁚

Margaret met Hammond Frank on the flight to Sydney. His blond hair was just a shade darker than hers; Handsome, he had an impish curl of the lips that grew when he laughed. They were sitting together on the flight from Los Angeles. They had hit it off. He had seen her studying her Australian bird guide and showed her his copy of the same guide. Maggie was enjoying the idea of her return to her native land as a birder, and she appreciated the special attention he gave her.

"I find the scent coming from your book provocative. What is it?" Frank asked.

"Oh, that's just jasmine. I've kept my bird guide next to a pot of jasmine. I grow it for good luck, and it's is often thought a symbol of love and a stimulant of the libido. Hank, my deceased husband, said it turned him on. We grew it inside and outside our house to enjoy its wonderful aroma."

He told her to call him "Porky."

"I see by your book you're a birder," he said. "I'm taking a birding tour. Are you planning to do birding in Australia?"

"Yes, I'm going on a long tour with Aussie Bird Tours."

"Great. Me too. We can help each other learn Aussie birds—a great way to pass the long hours of this flight." So they spent the travel time studying the bird plates in their field guides while getting to know each other. Porky introduced her to a game he named *What's that bird?*

"One person says, 'I'm thinking of a bird,' and the other asks a yes-or-no question to identify it. We'll have to play an open guide version since we don't know any Australian birds," Porky said. "You have to ask questions we can answer yes or no. She agreed, and he said, "I'm thinking of a bird." After about ten minutes, looking through her guide, she correctly guessed "Kookaburra.'"

Porky imitated the call described by his guide.

Margaret laughed as the people around them peered at him with looks of amazement and grumblings of disapproval.

"This seems like a good way to learn the birds," Margaret said, "but maybe we should be quieter."

'Okay, I didn't mean to embarrass you. What do you do besides watching birds?"

"I enjoy being a member of my garden club and Birds & Floats. That's a local environmental group trying to save land from development, but I miss my husband. Birding seems to help fill the void he left. I've just begun to list birds. I've been told that Australia is a great place to see many new birds fast. The beauty of birds appeals to me as much as flowers do. Looking through this guide confirms what I was told."

She was pleased that Porky seemed to find her attractive. She caught him admiring her figure. "I'm returning to my Australian homeland on this birding tour," she told her new friend. "I was still in school when Hank came out on a business trip. My father brought him home for dinner. We hit it off. He was a widower, and before he finished his business a week later, he asked me to marry him. My parents insisted I finish school, but Hank came back. I graduated one day and married him the next."

By the time they had finished over three days of birding trips around Sydney, Margaret had formed more than a casual acquaintance with "Porky" Frank. The group had listed over a hundred species of birds, including the well-named lyrebird, whose song had an ethereal quality that entranced Margaret. And they had seen many of the strange animals and sampled the aromas of the land down under by the time they reached Melbourne.

Chapter Two

Margaret realized that Porky was romancing her—she believed part of his purpose was to learn about Australia, but he made clear that he also desired her for herself. She was willing to admit to herself she enjoyed the admiration of such a good-looking admirer, whom she told to call her "Maggie.".

"All my close friends call me that."

Unaccustomed to so much recent attention from a male companion. Maggie was enjoying the tour. Her first negative revelation about Porky came on a field trip the day Porky tried to show off by telling her she was watching a swamp kangaroo. The guide corrected him. "Way too light—swamp kangaroos are dark brown. That was just a large gray eastern," he said. Porky covered his mistake by saying he should have used his binoculars. Her faith in his veracity was further shaken when she asked about his work. "Are you on vacation?"

Porky gave what she came to think his standard answer. "I do consulting work. I'm between jobs and exploring possibilities here." Maggie marked him down as a rolling stone, something she disapproved of. "My Hank ran a company. He believed in putting down roots."

Porky confirmed her distrust when he laughed. "I couldn't go on tours like this if I had too many roots, Maggie."

Still, she had found him pleasant company who could always come up with a funny comment or a story to pass the time. She had to laugh when he compared one of their tour leaders to a kangaroo and mimicked him, hopping about the group, all legs and ears.

One of the humorous stories Porky told her was of an Australian man who always ordered three draft beers. "An Aussie left Sydney and went to Melbourne," Porky said. "He went into a bar and ordered three draft beers at once. He took all three to a table and drank them one by one. "'Hey mate,'" the bartender said when the man asked for a refill. "'You should order and drink one draft at a time before it goes flat.'"

Other customers nodded. "I agree," the drinker said, but claimed he and his two brothers had made a pact when they left Sydney. "We'd drink this way in memory of each other."

Maggie interrupted. "So far I don't see anything very funny about drinking beer that way."

"Just wait,' Porky said. "This went on for several years until one day the Aussie ordered only two beers. The bar went quiet, and the bartender expressed his condolences. The beer drinker laughed. "You misunderstand. I just got married to a Baptist lady. I had to quit drinking—but my two brothers haven't quit.'"

Maggie laughed. "I guess your story was good to the last drink, but you took a long time getting to the funny part."

Nevertheless, some of Porky's jokes were a bit too risqué for Margaret's taste. She recalled Porky's joke about the best way to find a friendly Australian woman.

She had ventured, "I suppose you'd go to Australia."

He laughed. "That works to begin with, but the *best* answer is to look to see if she is 'down under'—under her man, that is. I'd like to show you sometime."

She laughed and challenged him. "Do you consider your-self a good lover?"

"Passable, I've received compliments."

"From inexperienced females, no doubt. If you were such a good lover, you wouldn't promote the missionary position."

He grinned. "You have me there, Maggie."

He was good company, though. Never a dull moment with Porky around, and after a week, she had tried him out with a little kissing and petting at first, then something more, but she made it a point always to avoid the missionary position. She thought him a poor substitute for Hank, but she couldn't help liking him; still, she thought him no Hank.

Porky did know how to arouse her passions. He offered her solace. Her single room gave them a privacy double occupancy precluded. Hank had always teased her about her proclivity for taking in strays, saying he figured that's why she'd married him. Porky was just another stray, she decided.

Porky became jealous when Jameson Kanger came to the tour as co-leader for the northern leg of the tour. He tried to invade what Porky had come to consider his personal territory. At first things went fairly well. Jameson knew the flora and fauna thoroughly, and for a while he pressed Margaret with attention despite Porky's jealousy, but he and Porky both began to ignore her when they found another project to share.

They soon were spending almost all of their spare time discussing this scheme, whatever it was, ignoring her. She suspected they were up to no good. For some reason their scheme, whatever it was, involved curlews, and Porky became very excited the two days the tour produced little curlews. She controlled her pique, however, because she didn't want to give up Porky's nighttime attentions, although these were decreasing in quality and number.

Chapter Three

So Maggie was often left to herself to form friendships with other members of the tour. Not one to sulk, Maggie made a lot of friends. One of them was especially close, Patricia Shaper, a fellow Galvestonian, whom she had met at Birds & Floats. She knew Patsy was an Olympic champion in Women's Trap Skeet and admired the younger woman's skill, good looks and well-formed figure. One morning Patsy appeared at breakfast a bit haggard, bags under her brown eyes, and rich brown hair unkempt. Maggie asked if she were ill.

"Not really, I went drinking with Kanger last night. It was a bummer. He drugged my drink and had sex with me—without my permission—the sonofabitch ignored my orders to stop. That bastard raped me. The drug made me weak."

"Honey, what a bastard. He may know his animals and plants, but he's not much of a man." Maggie put an arm around her friend and consoled her with a warm kiss on the lips.

Patsy hugged her in response and returned the kiss. "I should have known better, but he is handsome in a roguish way. Still, I don't like to be tricked into sex. Rape isn't my idea of good birding—or good sex."

Maggie caressed Patsy. "Honey, you just can't trust men. You spend the night with me tonight." Maggie knew what Patsy needed. She felt violated. She liked to be in control, and she'd lost control. Maggie knew she could provide Patsy with sympathy and a sense of control.

Patsy nodded. "I'd love to. Please keep between me and Kanger today. I'm afraid I might do something I'd regret. I can see the headline. 'Olympic champ brawls with tour leader'. It'll be too bad for Jameson if he ever crosses my path when I hold a loaded shotgun.'"

A few nights later, Patsy came to Maggie's room after supper; Maggie pulled out her bottle of gin and some tonic water and made them drinks. Then she excused herself and went into her bathroom. She came out wearing just a light see-through nightgown. Refilling their glasses with more gin and less tonic, she sat down beside Patsy. "I have another night-gown like this. Why don't you change into that, Dear? I'll help you forget what happened to you the night Kanger raped you."

Later, as they sat on the bed and admired each other's figures, Patsy gently pulled Maggie to her and kissed her. By morning the two women had formed a close friendship and didn't worry about being around Frank and Kanger anymore as long as they saw the strange animals the tour encountered.

Savoring her close friendship with Patsy, Maggie encour-aged her friend to accuse Kanger. "You should report him to the police."

Patsy shook her head. "It'll be my word against his in a foreign country."

During the following week, Patsy and Maggie kept as far away from Kanger and Porky as possible without miss-ing out on birds and other animals. By the time they reached Brisbane in Queensland, Patsy had recovered her self-assur-ance. She had decided not to press charges against Kanger.

"I want to spend my time enjoying the rest of the trip. I couldn't have much fun trying to bring Kanger to justice," she said, as she explained her decision to Maggie. "I'll take care of him when I fill out my sheet the company gives us to state our satisfaction with the trip. I will hint at the possibility of a lawsuit. You could mention his rape of me on your evaluation too. Those evaluations should end Kanger's career as a tour guide for Aussie Bird tours. That's some revenge. I'll still have the opportunity to do more later."

"It's your choice. I'll certainly back you up. I can understand you don't want to deal with it now and ruin the rest of this expensive trip. We've been having too much fun."

Maggie now abhorred Kanger and avoided Porky because of his connivance with the rapist. She devoted the rest of the trip to Patsy and the exotic birds. The strange mammals such as the platypus and kookaburras of this land down under entranced her.

∮　∮　∮

Hammond Frank was waiting at ten o'clock in the morning, eating brunch, at a barbecue place on the Seawall in Galveston when Mackensie Craft arrived for the meeting Margaret Smith had arranged for him with Porky. She had renewed her relationship with Porky when he showed up at her door unannounced soon after she returned from Australia. He apologized for neglecting her their last days on the tour. After they had a few glasses of wine and were back on good terms, Porky told her he was looking for people who'd pay a high fee to see an Eskimo curlew.

'You might talk to Mackensie Craft," Maggie said. "He's a well-heeled birder I met at Birds & Floats programs. He considers his life list of bird species a very serious matter. He has over 5,000 species and hopes to top Phoebe Snetsinger's list of over 8700. He's a rough fellow, though."

Just the sort of mark Porky was looking for: a rich guy obsessed with seeing as many of the world's bird species as possible, one who would pay a big fee to see the supposedly extinct Eskimo Curlew. Galveston Island was the site where the last authenticated sighting of the species had occurred. Now Porky and Kanger were claiming an Eskimo curlew sighting and were seeking a few obsessed listers who would pay well to see one. The sighting was not to be noised about. "Tell him the information is confidential, only for those who pay the fee," Porky said. Maggie agreed to arrange for Craft to meet Frank at a barbecue place on the Seawall. He was supposed to recognize Porky by the binoculars around his neck.

A heavy-set man about six feet tall with unkempt black hair and a matching beard came in about five minutes after ten and ordered a coffee at the counter. Surveying the room, he took his coffee and walked over to Porky's table. "Are you Hammond Frank?" he asked.

"That's right. Just call me Porky. You must be Mackensie Craft. Margaret Smith tells me you're a serious lister."

"I reckon so. I have over 5,000 species of birds on my life list. That's more than half the species of birds in the world."

"I've been told you might be willing to pay to see a really rare bird."

"I might. It would depend on how rare."

"How does Eskimo curlew sound? Rare enough?"

"Pretty rare—no authenticated records since 1963. But there have been lots of people claiming to have seen one since then—a lot on the upper Texas coast. The '63 record was right here on this island."

"Would it be worth ten thousand dollars to you to see one?"

"For that kind of money. I would want to see an unfettered wild bird and photograph it to support the observation."

"I'd want half up front and half after you see the bird. The photograph is not included. That's entirely up to you, but I don't want the bird spooked."

"Don't worry. I have a big lens. I don't have to get close, but I take pride in keeping a clean list. I don't want to be tricked. Maybe you haven't heard that people call me Mack the Knife? I got the name because of cutting up a few people who crossed me."

Reaching to his side, Mack pulled out a large hunting knife and brandished it a few inches from Porky's nose. "People who've crossed me have scars from this knife," he bragged. "If you're not honest about that curlew, you'd better back out now."

Covering his fear, Porky coughed and bargained. "Well, you can pay me a quarter up front and the rest after you see the bird, wild and unfettered. I repeat, getting the photo is your responsibility."

"If you really have located an Eskimo curlew, I'm willing to pay that much, but the record better be on the level. You'll pay with your hide if it isn't." Craft looked around to see if anyone was watching and then made a cutting gesture with his knife.

"Well, you need to act fast. No telling how long the bird will hang around. It's an Arctic migrant on its way north. Do you know the aquarium pyramid at Moody Gardens?"

"Sure, but I'm certain the bird's not there—no habitat."

"No—but bring your binoculars and camera and meet me in the parking lot for the aquarium pyramid in two hours. I'll show you where I found the curlew, but I want the down payment now. I'll give it back if we can't locate the bird."

"All right," Craft said and pulled out a wad of bills, divided it, and handed part to Porky. "Count it."

"I'll do that later; I have to go. I have another prospect to see before then. There're others who want to see the bird. Who knows when it'll take off for the Arctic?"

Porky rose to leave. He didn't want to press his luck with Craft's knife, but he didn't fear he'd use his knife in front of so many witnesses.

"**Don't** keep me waiting." Craft emphasized the negative as Porky walked away.

Frank hurried out the door and on to his next prospect.

Chapter Four

In the ramshackle police station of the City of Galveston, Texas, on a morning in 1994, two members of the department were discussing a major case. It was high on the list of problems Chief Jerold Henderson had asked them to review. They were going over the evidence they had for a serial rapist.

"The rape five nights ago is the second like it in three months. It's not what we're used to dealing with. Whoever this guy is, he's not leaving much evidence behind," Detective Robert (Bob) Bruce said. "He's a ghost roaming over Galveston like the hound of the Baskervilles, leaving no trace behind but fearful victims."

Bruce's companion, Sergeant Stephen Jackson, shook his head.

"I can't understand what pleasure a man gets from rape. I like for women to find me so desirable they encourage me to make love. He's no ghost. He's a clean-up freak. He makes his victims shower."

Bob nodded, "He's trying to erase all traces of rape. He cleans up. He's dressing all in black, threatens them with a knife and tells them he has a gun, rapes them, and then makes them shower. Not much else. We have a clever serial rapist on our hands." He drained his coffee cup and walked over to the machine to get another.

"Yeah, imagine making your victims shower. He's driving the Chief up the wall. The Mayor and the Council are all over him, and the Chamber of Commerce is worrying about the tourist trade. He's making life hot for us. I almost wish we had a murder to take the heat off," Jackson said as the odor of cigar smoke alerted them to the approach of Chief Henderson.

The smoker materialized in the five-foot eight corpulent bald form of Chief Henderson. "You boys have anything new on that serial rapist?" he asked as he filled a cup with coffee.

Detective Bob Bruce shook his head. "We don't have leads. All we have is the descriptions of his actions reported by his victims. He's obsessive in his efforts to avoid leaving any clues. He might as well be a lustful ghost."

Henderson blew a perfect smoke ring. "Well, keep looking. The damn Chamber of Commerce and a lot of big wheel asses are on my neck." Clamping his cigar back in his mouth, Henderson marched off to his office holding his coffee cup and trailing cigar smoke.

Coming past the Chief, Officer John Withers appeared and alerted them. "There's just been a report of gunshots out the West End on Settegast Road. A woman from something called Birds & Floats is demanding we investigate."

& & &

Summoned to a grassy field on the west end of Galveston by a woman cutting brush for Birds & Floats, Detective Bruce and Sergeant Jackson met the informant. She directed them to a large fog-covered field whose short-mown grass bordered a larger fog-covered section the mower had not touched. Searching near a copse of bushes and hackberry trees in the foggy area, the detectives found a horribly slashed body of a man. Looking at the blood-covered body, Steve Jackson shook his head as a metallic odor struck his nostrils. His stomach tensed as he fought an urge to puke his breakfast of eggs and bacon. He considered the urge as unbecoming a man given the nickname of his favorite Civil War hero, Stonewall Jackson. "It's a bloody mess. I wonder if those cranes over there saw the murder?" He couldn't help trying to joke. "They wouldn't make very good witnesses at a trial."

Putting on plastic gloves, Bruce examined the double-barreled shotgun Steve had found thirty yards from the body in the direction of the bay. Both barrels were empty.

"They're long-billed curlews, not cranes, but they tell us it's been some time since the murder. They would have flown away at the shots if they'd been here then," Bob said.

Steve nodded. He admired his fellow officer, a former hunter and a crack shot, who now hunted only with optics. Bob loved classical music, good literature, and natural history. Steve admired him on account of his shooting ability, intellect, and steady demeanor.

Steve scratched his forehead, "Why would somebody use a knife to cut up a person he'd already shot with a double-barreled shotgun?"

Bob Bruce looked up at a tall man in his late twenties. Six foot three Stonewall Jackson had not made Sergeant by being politically correct. A confirmed admirer of Robert E. Lee and a high school football star, his good looks and friendliness led women to ignore his old-school approach, and gained him some friends of questionable politics, but Bob had developed respect for his colleague's honesty and hard work.

Bob stood. "We have this shotgun and a pair of binoculars. Maybe we'll get an answer there. I don't know, maybe somebody wanted it to look like a crime of passion, but whoever it was seems to have been deliberate, more like an avenger than a murderer in fear of discovery. The shots caught the attention of that lady cutting brush, but she didn't see anybody. That's not too unlikely in this fog."

"Yeah, it's going to be difficult searching the area."

Bob checked his plastic gloves and turned the decedent's body over, showing the back slashed as well. "If it's a crime of passion, we have to find what could have angered the killer so much that he'd commit a murder and then desecrate the body like a madman." *God damn, what a bloody sight.* He turned his face away from the corpse.

Squatting by the body, across from Bob, Steve said, "I'm glad we don't get too many like this. It's not helping my digestion. I reckon the first thing to do is identify the corpse. The murderer did away with the victim's wallet, if he had one."

"Maybe the Medical Examiner can help us. We may need a DNA analysis. The face is too disfigured for photos to help much without some reconstruction. One thing that bothers me is that two shots were fired from the shotgun, but as far as I can tell, only one of them hit the murder victim."

"Okay, another thing, we can start by identifying the owner of this field. Maybe whoever it is knows our victim," Steve Jackson said, as he pulled out his cell phone and punched the number of the medical examiner's office. After talking with someone, he said, "The examiner's office has already been informed."

Bob nodded. "I know who owns this land—a non-profit organization called Birds & Floats. They lead kayak tours of the marsh and promote art, nature conservation, and bird and butterfly watching. They do a lot to educate kids and older people about the importance of nature. They're trying to save some of the island from development," Bob said as he pulled off his bloody gloves. "We'll ask Georgina Clayton. She runs Birds & Floats. She's a honey. Georgina will be glad to check what legal visitors they've had, but I'd bet we're looking for trespassers."

Turning from the curlews, Bruce pointed to a large bird perched in a tree whose leaves were beginning to bud. "That's an osprey perched there. Some people call them fish eagles. That's its *teec, teec, teec* call. You're a fisherman, aren't you?"

Steve nodded.

"That's some of your competition," Bob said. "You should watch them. They do pretty well catching fish, but they don't breed here, as far as I know; they're mainly winter residents. That one's a little late going north. They listened to the osprey call and the observed the curlews while waiting for the medical examiner.

Steve searched the sky. "Where're the vultures?"

"They don't often come to the island. Soaring birds don't like to fly over large bodies of water because it doesn't provide the thermals they need to soar. I think a dead body might attract a coyote, but I believe the murder happened little more than an hour ago. Hardly time for a coyote."

The detectives were interrupted by a Galveston County Medical Examiner, Dr. Emden Castro, a short woman with shoulder-length black hair and a clear olive skin. She and two male assistants arrived pushing a gurney with a body bag lying on it.

Emden joked. "You fellows have a bad habit of turning up dead bodies I have to take to my morgue. It hasn't been here long; the stench isn't bad," she said as the policemen led her to the body. Steve was pleased to see her again. She had been the examiner on an earlier case of his, and he was still ruing that he'd made no move to find out more about her.

"Get ready for a very unpleasant sight," Bob Bruce said as they approached the body. "Whoever did this was very angry and maybe a bit crazy—or wanted us to think so."

Even though she had been a medical examiner for three years, Bob thought Dr. Castro appalled by the bloody corpse. Her face became pale as she directed one of her assistants to take pictures of the body and the murder scene while the other began to prepare the corpse for the body bag.

"I'm glad I don't deal with something this gruesome every day. You guys sure know how to ruin the prospect of a tasty bacon and tomato sandwich."

"I reckon it's hard to get used to." Steve said.

"This is the part of my job I dislike. Once I get them drained and cleaned properly, I don't have any trouble with them." She set about suggesting more pictures of the crime scene and then had her helpers take the body to the van.

"We have no idea who the victim is," Bob Bruce said. "I'm counting on you to help us identify him, and if you could come up with some DNA evidence of his killer, too, that would be great."

"I'll do what I can. Whoever did this must have a screw loose."

"Bob's not so sure," Steve said. "He thinks somebody did this to make us think the killer is a madman. I'm glad you have assistants to help with this job, but it was your choice to let corpses in your life," Steve joked, not wanting to admit his attraction to her beauty.

Noting Emden's frown, Bob intervened. "We've found a pair of binoculars, so it's possible at least one of the people involved was interested in nature, maybe a birdwatcher."

Not taking Bob's hint, Steve persisted. "What prompted you to spend your time with dead people?"

Emden scowled. "I guess as a teenager I watched too many bloody movies about people killing other people with chain-saws." She imitated a person using a chainsaw. She calmed. "Seriously, I keep my mind cleansed with nature study. That's why I spend time kayaking. Birds & Floats has some really good programs. It's a shame somebody picked their land for this bloody murder."

Bob intervened again. "I'm going to ask Director Georgina Clayton to give me a list of people who've had legal entry to the Birds & Floats land, but maybe whoever did this wasn't a member."

Bob and Steve walked with Emden back to her van and waited while her assistants loaded the body. As they waited, Bob's phone rang. "The Chief has summoned us to a shooting downtown," Bob said after the call ended: "We'll have to survey the murder scene later." As they parted, Steve invited Emden to have lunch with them sometime to make up for their having ruined hers.

Emden overlooked her chagrin at Steve's obtuseness. "Sure, we can make a date when I've found out who your star victim is."

Bob and Steve weren't eager to leave the murder scene before making a thorough search of the area, but Chief Henderson didn't like to have his orders ignored. And the fog was a hindrance to a thorough search. "He says we can come back later to search here. I'll call Georgina and ask her to help me go over this area as soon as I can leave you to take care of the downtown shooting."

Steve lifted his arms to the sky. "Henderson worries too much about politics, but I reckon we'd better leave a thorough search until later."

"The Chief seemed a bit perturbed about our taking time off the rape case. I'll ask Georgina to talk to Henderson."

Steve shook his head. "How would that help?"

"Georgina's got a lot of pull, not to mention a lot of personal magnetism. Sometimes I hang around Boats & Floats just to talk to her. I'll ask her to help me search the area."

⁝ ⁝ ⁝

Answering Bob's call, Georgina looked over her calendar. "Well, my schedule says I'm free until three o'clock this afternoon."

"I'd like your help searching a crime scene on Birds & Floats land after I take care of another case. I'll come by your office and pick you up, if that's all right. I'll treat you to lunch at Nate's when we're through."

"Sounds exciting."

"I'll call to let you know when I'm on the way."

Two hours later, answering his knock, Georgina greeted him in her field clothes, ready to help.

"You must want to solve this case in a hurry," she said as she looked up into his hazel eyes with what Bob thought a rather appraising look. "That's all right with me. I want to help. I'll feel like an intern."

Bob shrugged. "I think the case will take a long time to solve. It has me puzzled, and I'd like to find out what happened," Bob said as he casually glanced at her fingers—no rings.

Adjusting her seat belt, Georgina looked over at Bob. "You don't need to take me to lunch—getting to watch you work is sufficient reward. I'd like to know what caused the murderer to use Birds & Floats land."

Bob wanted very much to have lunch with her. "Do you have something against Nate's? The food's good."

"No, I like Nate's, but I don't want you to feel obligated just because I've agreed to try to bring Henderson around."

"It's settled then. I'd like some company for lunch, and you've become my special assistant on this case. We'll have lunch at Nate's."

Georgina gazed about them with an air of satisfaction as they walked across the field toward the murder site, Bob thought. "I believe you like your job with Birds & Floats."

She laughed. "Is it that obvious? I like undeveloped land and being your assistant too."

"What prompts you to take a job that doesn't pay what you deserve?"

"What prompts you? The last time I looked, Galveston police officers weren't so high on the pay scale."

"No, the pay's not great, but there's a good deal of satisfaction in solving crimes."

"I can understand. I work the crossword puzzles in the paper. For me, there's great satisfaction in saving land valuable to wildlife from too much undisciplined development. Putting together tracts of land is like solving a jigsaw puzzle. Raising funds to buy a special tract isn't fun, but seeing the land remaining without buildings gives me pleasure."

Bob nodded. "I understand. I reckon I like identifying birds and other animals because it's puzzle solving. And crime work is too."

Arriving at the field where he and Steve had found the corpse, they began searching. "If you find something, perhaps a shotgun shell, don't touch it but tell me. I'll come and pick it up with gloves and bag it. We'll start where Steve and I found the corpse and move out in circles."

They had made about five tight circles when Georgina called to Bob. "I've found something."

She pointed to a feather. Bob slipped on plastic gloves, picked up the feather and bagged it. "You have sharp eyes," he said and watched her lips make the beginning of a smile.

Resuming their ever-widening circle, they moved quietly for over ten minutes. "Georgina, I've found a shotgun shell," Bob said. He put on gloves again, stooped, picked up the shell and bagged it. Georgina walked over. He lifted up the bag for her to see. "With any luck there'll be fingerprints on this."

Surveying the ground near them, Georgina pointed to a footprint in drying mud.

"Good spotting," Bob said. "I'll get someone out here to make a cast," He searched for a stick to mark the spot and placed a glove over the stick." Pulling out his cell phone, he called the station and asked Henderson to send someone to make a cast.

They looked a little farther out without success, and Bob suggested it was time to look on the other side of the trees and bushes. About three yards beyond the copse, the marsh began. In several places wax-myrtle bushes created a lane extending almost to the marsh. In the clearing between two thick growths of bushes, they found evidence of a boat having been pulled up from a path leading through the marsh grass to the bay. Near the bank, Bob noticed something dark poking from a clump of blue stem. He reached over with a stick and pulled it to him.

As the two of them examined what turned out to be a cage, Georgina pointed to a few more feathers inside it. Bob pulled on a glove to extricate them from the cage to bag. "A bird of some kind has been transported in this not too long ago. I don't have a bag large enough for the cage, so I'll just carry it with a gloved hand."

"What would anyone want with a bird cage out here?" Georgina asked.

"The answer must be connected to the feathers we've found."

They walked the rest of the way around the copse of hackberry, yaupon, and wax-myrtle without finding anything else until they reached the middle of the other side. There Bob spied some scattered millet and other seeds and pointed them out to Georgina.

. "It looks like somebody's been feeding animals here," Georgina said. "I find this strange, don't you?"

Putting down the cage and pushing into the brush, Bob pulled out a thin white rope attached to a bush. He detached it and noticed a clasp on each end. "It appears that something, a bird or other animal, was kept here."

"Do you think it's connected to the murder?"

"I think it must be, but I'm not sure how," Bob said as he bagged the rope, picked up the cage, and started to his car.

Chapter Five

Later, as Bob was putting the new evidence in his trunk with care, another police car drove up, and Sgt. Jackson and Officer John Withers got out.

"Where did you find that cage?" Steve asked, as Bob pointed his colleague toward the marked footprint.

"On the other side of the thicket. It had some feathers in it."

"Feathers?"

"Yes, Georgina found another feather over here, and she found the footprint we need to make a cast of. It should make a good cast."

"I brought John to make the cast," Steve said.

Georgina, do you know Sgt. Steve Jackson and Officer John Withers? Steve's my sidekick and John is our fingerprint expert."

"It's a pleasure to meet both of you."

Steve shook Georgina's hand. "Good to meet you too, Georgina. You're the head of Birds & Floats, Bob says. You've helped us with a political problem. Thanks."

Georgina grinned. "*De nada.* It was my pleasure. Your chief can be a little pompous, but he means well."

As soon as Bob had introduced Georgina to Steve and John, Bruce and Georgina left. "I'll fill you in on what we found later today, Steve," Bob said. "Right now I'm taking Georgina to the lunch I promised her."

Bob drove slowly to Nate's along Stewart Road so that he and Georgina could watch the birds on the wires and in the ditches. "Look, there's a kingfisher on the wire and mottled ducks in the ditch," Georgina said. Down the road a little, she spied a kestrel hovering. "It hovers just like its European cousin. That's why it's called the windhover. The English poet Gerard Manley Hopkins wrote a beautiful poem about its cousin."

"Daylight's dawn-drawn falcon," Bob quoted, as he pulled into a parking place at Nate's.

"A policeman who quotes poetry; you have hidden talents. I'm pleased you didn't hide them from me. We have a lot in common." She smiled and put her hand on his.

"Consider it a verbal appetizer." Bob said.

Bob ordered a draft beer and a bowl of gumbo while Georgina asked for a shrimp poorboy and a glass of red house wine. As they settled down to eat, Georgina asked, "Do you have any theories about the murder?"

"I'm sure it's something much more unusual than the ordinary scam Frank used. It must have been especially difficult and lucrative. And somehow it involved birds."

"None of that explains the bloody corpse you've told me about. It sounds like the work of a madman," Georgina said.

"I know, but somebody might have done it to mislead us. We'll have to find out more in order to figure out what Frank was doing. I'm going to send those feathers we found to the Smithsonian for identification. It might help if we know what bird they belonged to. And I'm going to have the shotgun and shell examined for fingerprints and DNA."

"I hope you'll keep me abreast of developments. Because the murder was on Birds & Floats land, I guess I feel a little like it's our murder. I want to catch the knife wielder. I'm enjoying being your special assistant," Georgina said as she bit into her poorboy. Bob thought to himself how lucky he was to have an excuse to be with Georgina.

As he sampled his bowl of gumbo, Bob nodded. "You've been such a great help with the case, how could I refuse you? I need you to handle the Chief, and it's obvious that you have great eyesight. Don't worry; I'll keep you up-to-date."

Back at the station, after he had taken Georgina to her office, Bob filled Steve in on what he and Georgina had found, and, after going over all of the clues they had, the men agreed they had to have a great deal more evidence. They concurred on looking over the shotgun and shell for fingerprints and sending the feathers to the Smithsonian. And when Emden had Frank's face ready, they would ask Georgina for an identification.

₭ ₭ ₭

He didn't get to call her. Once the answer to the identification of the victim reached her, Dr. Emden Castro called the police.

"Detective Bruce here."

"This is Emden. I sent off samples for DNA analysis in an effort to detect the killer as well as the victim. I have some news for you. I've found the identity of your bloody victim from his DNA. Is the offer for lunch still open?"

"I reckon, if you can put up with just me. Steve's on another assignment elsewhere this afternoon. How would you like to go to Benno's? We can sit outside and watch the laughing gulls and pelicans fly over—might even see a dolphin break water."

"Sounds great. I need to see some live animals and people.

"Last annual check-up I had, the doc said I was alive and well."

She consulted her appointment book. I'll meet you at Benno's. I haven't eaten there, but I think I know where it is." She looked at the city map on her wall. "About 13th on the Seawall, isn't it? Okay. What time? That's great. I'm flexible. My clients don't demand I keep a tight schedule." She doffed her white coat and left after hanging it up.

Emden was standing by the entrance to Benno's when Bob arrived, parked, and walked over.

"It's good to see you so soon again. It's just as well Sgt. Jackson wasn't available. I might not have agreed to lunch if he had been," Emden said.

Bob grinned. "Steve lacks polish. Sometimes he lives up to his nickname of Stonewall, but he means well. For some people he's an acquired taste, but most of them grow to like him. "

Looking up into Bob's tanned face and hazel eyes, she smiled. "Well, if he overcomes my opinion of him, he'll have become an acquired taste, but I'm looking forward to lunch with a live person. I usually have a sandwich in my office, just down from the corpses."

He held the door for her as he directed her to the line of people waiting to order. Bob saw amazement in Emden's face.

"Is there always a crowd this big?"

"Usually. Holidays are the worst. We stand in line at the bar to order; the menu's on the board behind the counter."

"What do you recommend?"

"If you like Cajun and oysters, you should try their Cajun oyster plate. I'm having that with a draft of Shiner Boch. You just get your drink and give your order. Then find a table. I'll get our number. They'll bring our order to us. Would you like to sit outside?"

"Yes, the weather's fine."

Emden picked a table. "How's this? It has a good view of the Gulf.

Bob had their service number: 16. Emden had chosen the Cajun oysters, but she asked for water. Bob sniffed. "Smell that sea air, and there's a flotilla of pelicans soaring by, not moving a wing."

He took a sip of his draft beer, savoring its fruity bite. He pointed to a dolphin breaking water. "Watch for the dolphins," he said. "Since this is supposed to be a business lunch, I reckon you'd better tell me what you've found out about the bloody corpse before the food comes. We don't want to ruin a good meal."

Their oysters arrived at this point, just in time. Bob's stomach was beginning to complain.

"Let's do justice to these oysters," Bob said

Not long after they'd begun eating, Emden said, "Ooh…a great choice, they're delicious. Umm. these *are* tasty. These mollusks practically melt in your mouth. I can't eat all of mine, now, though."

"We'll get a box," Bob said. "You can have what's left of yours for supper."

"That's a great idea."

After a few more bites, she turned to business. "The victim was from the Midwest, St. Louis, Missouri. His name is Hammond Frank, a career confidence man. I sent off some things I thought might have DNA of the killer, but I haven't heard back yet. That will take more time."

Bob lifted his draft before responding. "Well, that's good work. Did you turn up anything else?"

"Yes, I did, but it may not mean anything. I found some snippets of paper torn by the knife but still together more than enough to show they were about a bird called the Eskimo curlew."

"That's a rare bird, probably extinct."

Emden's face had a puzzled expression. "What could that have to do with the murder?"

"One of the last confirmed sightings of the Eskimo curlew was on Galveston Island in 1963. Maybe the victim was a birdwatcher. Why would somebody kill a birdwatcher over an Eskimo curlew? That's hard to figure."

"Well, it's a place to begin. You're the detective." She handed him the pieces of the brochure. "He's *your* confidence man."

"Well, thanks for your help. By the way, don't be too harsh on Stephen. He's just a little behind the times. He's an unreconstructed Confederate."

Emden laughed. "Oh, I don't mind him too much. He's a lot like my dad—left over from the last century. I'm out of place in the morgue according to him too."

"Things are changing fast, too fast for some of us, including my boss. My chief 's objecting to the time Steve and I are spending on this case. He thinks we should be trying to find the serial rapist who's causing us bad publicity. Henderson worries too much about politics, but I think we can handle that problem."

⅋ ⅋ ⅋

As Steve and Bob walked by their boss's office next day after Bob had asked for Georgina's help, Chief Jerold Henderson motioned the detectives in. After taking a puff on his cigar, the Chief asked, "Have you made any progress on that murder out on Birds & Floats' land?"

Bob forced himself not to smile. "No, I haven't devoted much time to that case. Remember, you told us not to."

"Yeah, I remember, but I've changed my mind. Don't neglect your other cases, especially the serial rapist, but give the Frank murder high priority."

"Okay, it's going to take some time, I think."

Chief Henderson took another puff on his cigar. "Just keep me informed of your progress."

"Sure thing. We've found out that the murdered guy is Hammond Frank, a confidence man from St. Louis." Bob said. as he and Steve turned back into the hall, aware that they owed Georgina Clayton a favor.

Chapter 6

The next day Bob asked their best fingerprint man, John Withers, to search the cage and shotgun, When the results came back, Bob could hardly bring himself to accept them. Three sets? Two would have been enough, but three? He raised his coffee cup and saluted Withers. "*Slan ge vah*. Are you sure?"

John Withers laughed. "If you think that's amazing, listen to this. Only one of the sets was on the cage."

Bob took a long drink of coffee. "Damn, not much help there. We have to find out about those bird feathers."

"As you requested, I've sent them off to the Smithsonian," Withers said. "We should get an answer in a couple of weeks, if we're lucky and they take it up immediately. This is not an easy task. There're not that many people in the world who could do it. The lady at the Smithsonian is one in a million, according to her reputation."

Bob drained his cup and poured another. "I'll call Emden and ask her to send over a copy of Frank's fingerprints to compare with what we have on the shotgun," he said. "That way we'll know if his prints are one of the three sets we have on the gun."

Steve laughed. "Why not go see her. Take your Cannon camera and photograph Frank, if she has the face in decent shape. I'll go if you don't want to. I admire her, in spite of her attraction to dead men."

"No, I'll go. You're right. We need the picture to show Georgina. Do you want to go too?"

Steve tapped Bob on the shoulder. "I'll be glad to tag along."

Bob called to let Emden know he and Steve were on their way to her lab to take a picture of Frank's face and to get a copy of his fingerprints.

"I was wondering when I'd hear from you," Emden said. "You have good timing—I finished prettying him this morning. I'll make a copy of his prints for you while you're on your way."

Occupied with Georgina and the survey of the murder site, Bob had had little time to think about Emden, but he remembered how beautiful she was even as she examined the bloody corpse of Hammond Frank. Seeing her again in her lab coat confirmed his memories of her appeal. He could see why Steve appreciated her beauty. "Thanks for repairing Mr. Frank," Bob said as she met them in the hall leading to the morgue.

Emden waved her hand as if brushing the favor away as they walked into the quiet home of the dead. "I hope Mr. Framk looks enough like himself to lead to an ID. He's not too handsome now, but he probably had sex appeal when he was alive."

Bob readied his Cannon camera with its close-up lens as Emden pulled out Frank's body. He looked at the dead man's face. Damn! The face looked familiar. "Crap, Emden I've seen this guy. He volunteered at Birds & Floats. You sure did a great job. I don't know what name he was using, but the people at Birds & Floats may be able to match him with their list of members."

After Bob snapped photos, Emden began to shove Frank's body back into its assigned space. "I'm glad to have been of help," she said. Leading them back into her office, she handed Steve a plastic bag containing copies of Frank's fingerprints. Bob thought he detected a glow on her face as she handed over the prints to Steve.

"I think such good work deserves a reward," Steve said. "If you aren't busy, how about dinner tonight?"

Emden hesitated, looking down at the corpse.

Bob thought she must remember some of Steve's politically incorrect remarks. "I'm sure Steve would be on his best behavior," he said.

Emden still hesitated, "I don't think Mr. Frank would mind, but I think you and I got off on the wrong foot the other day, Steve."

Steve realized he had offended her. "I apologize. I promise to be more careful with my humor in the future. I admire you. I didn't mean to offend you."

Emden looked up from the corpse and smiled. "I accept your apology—and your dinner invitation.

"Would six o'clock and Benno's suit you?"

She nodded, laughed, and finished pushing Frank into his assigned spot. "I like Benno's, and I'm sure the Galveston police do too."

"You'll have to give me an address so I can pick you up."

"Come here. I'll meet you out front."

Steve wondered whether Emden was working late or didn't want him to know where she lived. He respected a woman who was careful with a man she didn't know well.

Back at the station, over coffee, Bob planned his afternoon. "I'll call Georgina and see if she's free to look at a photograph in an hour or so. I hope she can give us a name. If she can't, maybe somebody else there can, I know Frank volunteered at Birds & Floats. I saw him. You want to go along? We'll make a copy of Frank's picture at the station before we go."

"Okay, great, maybe we'll get a break."

Bob gave Frank's fingerprints to their print expert.

"John, give these a going over. Try to match them with one of the three you got off of the shotgun. Steve and I are going to see if Georgina can give us some information to go with Frank's photo."

Withers held the prints up for a better look. "I'll get right to these. I'll let you know when you get back."

A call to Birds & Floats revealed Georgina's location—out at the west end Birds & Floats land. "She'll meet us at the road near the murder site. You drive while I go over this list she gave us. I may know some of them. If she can't match a name on the list with the photo, we'll stop by their office and ask whoever's there."

Ten minutes later, as they pulled up to where Georgina waited along the fence.. "I'm sure she looks good in any-thing," Bob said. Steve nodded and laughed. "I think you have more than a casual interest in her."

Both Bob and Steve were glum when Georgina couldn't match the photo with a name on the list. "I'm disappointed too," she said. "I remember the face, but I can't help you with a name. He must have been a volunteer who worked on very few projects. You'll have to ask the people at the office."

"Is it possible that he wasn't a member?" Bob asked." I thought all your volunteers who work a certain number of hours are considered members."

"That's true, but if some people just come and help a few hours, one or two, without staying to the end of the work ses-sion, they could escape being counted."

"We can't rule out people who aren't on this list then," Steve said as he took the roll from her.

"No, I guess not, especially if they didn't want to be counted," Georgina said. "If I were planning something ille-gal, I wouldn't advertise my plans or my name."

"We'll pass the photo around your office and ask, if that's all right with you. If none of the people there can recall him, that'll indicate Frank was a non-member involved with some sort of scam." Bob waved goodbye as they were getting in their car and was happy to see her wave back.

Nobody at the office had luck matching the photo with names on the list, but several people recalled seeing him and remembering his name as Porky. Bob suspected a nickname based on Frank's name of Hammond. "It makes sense he'd conceal his real name if working on a scam and pretending to be a helper to gain access to the land without raising suspicion."

Back at the station, John Withers had interesting news. "None of the sets of fingerprints from the shotgun and cage matched those of Frank."

Slapping his thigh in obvious disgust, Bob evaluated this fact. "It's likely that he had a helper or helpers with the scam then. Some of those fingerprints could belong to them. Frank must have been the mastermind of a scam that went wrong."

Withers nodded and added, "That's not all. A kayaker has found another corpse in the marsh at the Birds & Floats land—near your murder site. You need to get back out to the end of Settegast Road."

They found the kayaker waiting for them, pushing a body toward shore. Catching sight of them, the paddler stopped. Bob smelled something foul when he sniffed the air. As the two policemen watched, the kayaker took off her headgear and revealed Georgina Clayton "Hey, you fellows need to find out who's littering Birds & Floats with dead bodies."

"We're trying. Just keep finding bodies. We think there might be one or two more," Bob said. "How did you happen to find him?"

"I began making my weekly survey of our marsh after you left me. About an hour later, I saw this body lodged against heavy marsh growth close to open bay, looking like it might be about to float into deep water. I called 911 on my cell phone; then I pushed the body toward the road. I was afraid it would be lost in the bay—lucky the water was so high I could push it in close here."

"We'll keep it here until the medical examiner arrives," Bob said.

"Okay, please keep me in the loop," Georgina said as she paddled off.

Half an hour later, the two policemen greeted Emden Castro and her assistants as they drove up to take charge of the corpse. "You guys are keeping the GCMEO busy. What do you have for me this time?".

Bob shrugged. "It's floating out there." Bob pointed to the floating body. Emden's assistants pulled on high boots, entered the water, and pulled the body in as Emdem and Steve rolled a gurney over to the edge of the road so that they could lift the body onto it.

"Doesn't look like a simple drowning," Emden said as she examined the body. "He has a deep head wound."

Bob nodded. "You think it may be related to the Frank murder."

"From the looks of the body, I guess he's been in the water several days at least," Emden said.

Steve grunted. "He's been somewhere long enough to smell rank."

"Okay, we'll take him in. I'll give you a preliminary report when you pick me up this evening," Emden said. Steve nodded.

As the van left with the body, Bob grinned. "Looks like you're working overtime tonight."

Chapter Seven

Emden was waiting in front of her office building when Steve arrived at six o'clock. She had on a black pants suit that showed her figure well and matched her pageboy hairstyle with bangs. "You certainly look attractive tonight." He restrained himself from saying, "*You look cute enough to make those clients of yours sit up and take notice.*"

"I didn't dress up for my clients, Sergeant," Emden said with a mischievous grin, as if she knew what he was thinking.

Amazed, Steve could hardly believe what he heard. *She can read my mind.*

In line at Benno's, Steve called Emden's attention to the aromas from the kitchen while they made a long wait. From the menu board on the wall behind the counter, Emden ordered a Cajun shrimp po'boy and a lemonade, and Steve ordered the Cajun oyster plate and a draft of Shiner Boch. Steve picked up their number, and they took their drinks outside. "You're fond of Cajun oysters," Emden said as they picked a table outside.

"I'm afraid to eat them raw anymore, and I don't like them fried the way they're usually fried, but I truly love Benno's Cajun oysters. I can't bring myself to order anything else here."

"I know they're good, but I thought I'd try something else to test Benno's."

"I'm sure you'll find the shrimp delicious too."

Looking up at the full moon hanging like a big ornament in the evening sky, Emden sighed and then turned her gaze to Steve.

"Are you and Bob making any progress with the Frank murder investigation?"

"I'm not certain. It grows more complicated every day. We have to figure out what Frank was up to with the Eskimo curlew brochure. That bird is probably extinct. It's hard to imagine a bird becoming extinct in a few short years. Georgina says there were millions of them alive in the 1870's."

"That's what happened to the passenger pigeon. Market hunters thought there was no end to them and killed so many there weren't enough left to breed," Emden said.

"People are too greedy, I reckon. They aren't the good stewards of earth God wants them to be," Steve said. "Real hunters take more care than money-hungry market hunters."

"The body from the marsh is indeed another murder victim, knocked unconscious, and left to drown. Drowning was the cause of death, but without treatment the head wound would have been enough to kill him." She handed Steve a plastic bag containing a set of fingerprints. "You'll be needing these to compare with those you have."

"Thanks, I hope this copy matches one of our sets. We're going to need a DNA analysis or something else to identify the guy."

"That breeze from the sea feels good," Emden said.

"Yeah, it brings a whiff of the ocean's saltiness in."

Their conversation was temporarily halted by the arrival of their food. "It smells good," Steve said. "But I'm hungry enough to wrestle a pelican for a fish."

By the time they were finishing their meal, the evening was darkening and Venus was visible. The ambience of the setting and the company were so pleasant, Steve ordered a second draft.

"The moonlight over the ocean whitecaps this evening is very romantic," Emden said as she watched a flock of pelicans soaring out to hunt a late evening meal. "It's amazing the way those birds drop down so straight into the water. I think they must enjoy dive-bombing into the ocean even when they don't catch a fish."

"I guess it takes a lot of practice. Where do you live, Emden? On the island?"

"No, I live with my family in Pasadena. It's a long drive, so many nights I sleep over at GCMEO. It's very quiet, and I have a pull-down bed. I keep everything else I need in my office."

Steve tossed a bit of bread to a great-tailed grackle looking up to him with a cocked head and a pleading yellow eye. "Are you safe at night?" he asked

"I have a key to the front door, and the night watchman checks on me before he locks up. I've thought of finding an apartment in Galveston, but that's expensive, and I still have a lot of school debt to pay."

The meal done, except for his beer, Steve disposed of their trash in the nearest bin. and sat back down. "Would you like to drive down to the beach and watch the tide and the moonlight shining on the beach? Or would you rather not?"

Emden smiled. "The beach sounds pleasant, and the moonlight is alluring."

At the eastern end of the seawall, Steve turned down Boddecker Drive, and when he reached the beach, he turned left and drove onto the packed sand and parked. They could look out over the Gulf. Under the moonlight, laughing gulls flying above screamed and black-crowned night herons hunched on posts in shallow water, waiting patiently, still as statues, hoping for a fish or a crab.

The sky was clear and the full moon was very bright. It shed light on the white cresting waves as they broke upon the beach and spread foam over the sand in front of them, leaving a sheen of wetness when it receded.

"Let's get out and walk on the beach a little," Emden said.

Steve nodded, and they were soon walking together toward the ocean on the packed sand, savoring the breeze and the salt air from the ocean. Steve delighted in Emden's warm touch as she took his hand in hers. When they stopped a few feet from the water line. Steve pointed out the man in the moon. "The old guy is really shining bright for us tonight."

Emden sighed. "Look how the moonlight glistens on the wet sand. It's beautiful."

Steve agreed with a kiss, and Emden twisted her tongue with his.

⁖ ⁖ ⁖

Next morning, over coffee, Steve gave Bob the bag with the fingerprints Emden had given him. Bob passed them on to John Withers and asked him to try to match them with a set of what they had begun to term the mystery prints.

"Have you heard anything from the Smithsonian?" Steve asked Withers.

"No, it's too soon, but they promised me they'd put it at the top of the list for identification. Stray feathers are not easy to identify. They have some experts—one woman is especially good—but they get lots of requests."

Bob poured himself a fresh cup of coffee. "Did you tell them Eskimo curlew needs not to be ruled out?"

Withers laughed. "Yeah, the guy said, 'In your dreams. I can tell you now they're not from an ivory-billed woodpecker.'"

Bob kicked his desk leg. "Eskimo curlew is a lot more likely than an ivory-bill on the island. We need to know what bird those feathers came from."

Steve paced around the office a bit, poured himself some coffee, and asked, "What if a member of Birds & Floats was involved with the scam Frank was working?"

"What makes you think that?" Bob asked.

"Just a hunch, considering a possibility. Not aware of the whole scam maybe, but involved some way, and perhaps owner of one of the sets of fingerprints we are wondering about."

Bob could smell the acrid odor of the Chief's cigar. "We need to make some progress. I reckon we might fingerprint all of the members and employees of Birds & Floats. We'd better ask Henderson's and Georgina's permission for that."

Soon after the cigar smoke arrived, the Chief appeared. "Are you two making any progress with that murder out at Birds & Floats? Ms. Clayton asked me about that last night at a fund-raiser."

"We're following a lot of leads," Bob said, sipping his coffee. "We think the corpse Ms. Clayton found might be involved with whatever scam Frank was working.

Bob stood. "Steve has a hunch maybe somebody at Birds & Floats might be involved. We need your approval and Ms. Clayton's approval to fingerprint her members and employees."

"If Ms. Clayton approves, I'll go along." Henderson said as he blew a perfect smoke ring over Bob's head. "I don't want to do anything she disapproves of unless it becomes absolutely necessary."

"Withers is looking at the drowned man's fingerprints for a match with those we already have from the Frank murder. We could ask Ms. Clayton for permission to fingerprint her members and employees," Bob said. "We'll need DNA or some other way to identify the guy."

"Do what's needed, but don't be too hasty. Ms. Clayton is worried. She thinks the Frank murder will hurt her fund-raising, if it hangs on."

That afternoon, Withers reported the results of his fingerprint comparison to Bob and Steve. "There's no doubt about it. The drowned man's fingerprints match the one we found on the cage and one of those on the shotgun. This guy's connected with the Frank murder."

"Thanks, now we have something to go on to solve this puzzle," Bob said. "I'll call Georgina and set up a meeting with her. You call Emden and tell her we need that guy identified as soon as possible."

The next afternoon, Bob and Steve met with Georgina at her office. Bob couldn't help noticing an enticing scent surrounding them. After sitting and taking the coffee she offered them, Bob explained that they might want to fingerprint the members and employees of Birds & Floats.

"Steve has a hunch that a member or employee of Birds & Floats is somehow involved with whatever scam Hammond Frank created. The dead man you found probably was working with Frank."

Georgina shifted in her chair and shook her head. "Are you sure of this? That's a lot to ask. Besides, if we do this, won't that alert whoever the person is?"

"Yes, that's why we want you to help us do it in a clandestine way. You must have standard questionnaires we could use to create a flyer to collect prints and other information about this new dead guy," Steve said.

Bob took a sip of coffee. "What's that pleasant fragrance I smell? Are you wearing perfume?"

Georgina laughed and pointed to a vase with jasmine branches. That's the scent of jasmine. I love it."

Bob grinned. "It seems to affect the libido."

Georgina laughed. "Yes, it's supposed to do that. It's also supposed to bring good luck. Are you feeling any of its power?"

"I'm not sure, but I hate to mention our reason for being here. The second victim's fingerprints do show he was involved with Frank. We need to identify our second corpse. What if we make a flyer with his photo on it asking your members and employees to report whether or not they've seen this man around Birds & Floats—and ask his name. Then ask them to sign and return the flyer with their answers to your office?"

Georgina laughed and pointed at Bob. "That's devious. What about people who don't reply?"

"You can demand your employees turn the flyer in. The employees and members who don't respond after a follow-up request will go on a list for us to investigate," Bob said.

Georgina nodded. "I'll give you one of our flyers to copy. Get me your flyer with a photo. I'll make copies and send them out. I do want to know if any of our people are involved."

"If we're right, one or two of them might be murderers," Steve said.

Chapter Eight

Bob and Steve spent the rest of the afternoon creating the flyer. While Steve worked on the form, Bob took his camera and drove to the medical examiner's office to take a photo of the drowned man. He called ahead to ask Emden to work some of her magic on the face of the deceased.

"I know it's short notice, but we want to create a circular with his picture on it. I'll explain when I get there."

Emden laughed. "I'll do my best. I'm not a make-up artist."

When Bob saw her handiwork, he grinned. "He looks like a poster boy," Bob said as he took several pictures. "He couldn't have been a leading man, but he could have been a star villain."

Looking on as Bob took pictures, Emden offered new information. "I checked on his clothes. They were made in Australia. A quick analysis suggests he might be part Australian aborigine. Does that help?"

"Interesting, it may help, especially if he's an Australian national. Maybe we can track him through immigration records. And it suggests that we should trace Hammond Frank's movements to see if he's spent any time in Australia during the last few years.

"I hope it helps. The Aussie drowned, but he might have as easily died of the head wound. Without attention, he certainly would have died from that."

Bob finished taking photos and showed them to Emden. "Good enough for an ID, I think."

"I'll keep working on his identity."

"You've given us another lead. It may help solve the puzzle. We need to know more about this man." Bob smacked his forehead with his open palm, as if just recalling something. "Have you established whether the shotgun wound or the subsequent knife wounds caused Frank's death? "

"Why?"

"It's possible we may have at least two killers on our hands."

"Either could have killed him, but the shotgun wound came first."

Putting his camera in its case, Bob went to his car and drove back to the station, He filled Steve in on what Emden had told him, and Steve agreed they should check immigration records. "I also think we should check with Georgina about any employees or members who have connections to Australia," Steve said.

By the next afternoon, the flyer with a picture of the suspected Aussie was ready to be taken to Birds & Floats for copying and distribution. Bob handed the sheet directly to Georgina in private so that nobody would know the police had had a hand in its creation. He again noticed how pretty she looked.

When she invited him to sit down and have some coffee, Bob accepted the invitation with alacrity. "I have some news you need to know. It may help you identify our second corpse. We've discovered the body you found is probably at least part Australian aborigine. So you might take a second look at anybody with Australian connections or has been to Australia lately."

"You're making progress. I'm so happy to be assisting you."

"You certainly convinced Jerold Henderson these murders are important. I think we have two bodies connected with Frank's scam, whatever it was, and I believe we may have two murderers."

"Then somebody other than our Aussie killed Frank?"

Bob was excited that they had figured out much of what was going on. "Yes, and no. I think whoever killed our Aussie also had a go at Frank, but I suspect somebody else had a hand in killing Frank. We have three sets of fingerprints to deal with."

Georgina nodded. "It's complicated."

"Yeah, and Frank may have had an unwitting helper who shared in the profits from the scam. But at least one of the victims of the scam was a poor loser. For some reason—money, or something else I haven't thought of—one scam victim was so enraged he killed Frank and his assistant."

"If you're correct, this is a complicated case. It's a puzzle crying to be solved."

"Georgina, that's an understatement. If you're not busy tonight, would you discuss this with me over dinner at Nate's?"

"What a great idea. I'll be through here by six. Why don't you pick me up at my home around six thirty?"

"You're on. You'll have plenty of time to see about getting those flyers out, and I'll have time to make a reservation."

At half past six o'clock, Bob knocked on Georgina's front door. The woman who opened the door had changed from field clothes and was attired in a tight blouse and jeans that gave the impression she had been poured into them. She was wearing a white jacket and semi-high heels that brought her face close to Bob's eye level. Looking at the beauty in front of him, Bob was glad he had put on a jacket. If he had known what a fashionable woman he was picking up, he'd have put on a tie too.

He stood speechless for a few moments. Georgina laughed. "You've never seen me in anything but field clothes. I hope you're not disappointed."

"Certainly not, but I admit to not expecting such a transformation. What a gorgeous creature I'll be escorting."

Georgina smiled—what Bob suspected was a smile of triumph—as he held his car door open for her. The drive to Nate's in the last rays of sunshine as the sun sank in the west showed a richly colored pink, gold, and blue sunset.

Georgina craned forward to see the sunset. "Red sky at night, a sailor's delight. How do policemen feel about beautiful sunsets?"

Feeling called upon for gallantry, Bob said, "They are especially fond of them when accompanied by a gorgeous woman."

"I'm pleased to hear that."

As they drove through Galveston Island State Park, Georgina saw a white-tailed kite hovering close to the highway. She pointed to it. "There's a kite looking for a cotton-rat supper."

"I think I'll wait for seafood at Nate's," Bob said.

On the other side of Jamaica Beach, they turned in to the drab building that was surrounded by elevated wooden steps leading to a door on the right and to an outdoor porch on the left. The parking area in front was filled with vehicles,

"I'm glad we don't have to wait," Bob said.

Inside, Nate's offered a plain area filled with tables and chairs—as crowded as usual. It was obvious that good food was what made Nate's popular. Bob was thankful he'd called ahead and made reservations. They were ushered to the table with a view of the ocean he had requested.

Besides water, Bob ordered a bottle of the house red wine. Georgina did not object. She recalled the house wine she had had the first time they had eaten at Nate's. "Have you thought more about our case?" she asked as she sipped her wine.

Bob sighed. "I'm still wrestling with the Eskimo curlew."

Georgina put down her wine. "I like this. It's a smooth table wine. What's puzzling you?"

Bob looked about to make sure nobody could hear them. "I think we're making progress on the Frank case, but I'm not sure yet about the connection of the Eskimo curlew brochure to the other clues we've discovered."

Leaning forward so that he could keep his voice low, Bob asked a question. "You're familiar with the birding crowd. What do you think a connection with the curlew could be?"

Georgina took Bob's hand in hers and pulled him closer. "Not only in touch with birders, I am one. Some listers are fanatics. They would pay big money to see a live Eskimo curlew in the field, wild, unhindered, to count for their list of species seen—what we call a life list. "

"Why pick your lands for the scam?"

"If I were going to develop a scam involving an Eskimo curlew, I'd pick Galveston Island or somewhere near, as the location to use—a place like our Birds & Floats land. Galveston is where one of the last confirmed records of a wild live Eskimo curlew took place."

Bob took a sip of wine. "I have seen plovers, upland sandpipers, and long-billed curlews on Birds & Floats land."

"Yes, it's the sort of place you'd expect to find an Eskimo curlew or some other shorebird that likes short grass, but almost everyone is beginning to believe the Eskimo curlew species is extinct. Though there are still many people who claim to have seen one, there's been no other confirmed record since 1963."

"How much do you think a well-to-do birder obsessed with his list might pay to see a live, unfettered Eskimo curlew?"

Bob refilled Georgina's glass with wine. "Five or ten thousand dollars," she said.

"That's certainly more than enough to attract a professional con man like Frank. You'd have a difficult time finding a more lucrative scam, but how does one find a live Eskimo curlew to use for a scam?"

Bob's question went unanswered as their food arrived. They both began with a cup of gumbo and proceeded to the blue crab special with asparagus and wild rice. By the time they finished, they had emptied their first bottle of wine. For dessert they split a slice of key lime pie.

Bob ordered another bottle of wine. They took their time finishing the pie.

"Why do people value wild creatures so much when rhey're down to a few specimens. It would have made more sense to protect them when there were stil thousands around. People are sure funny," he said.

"Would we value diamonds so much if we could find them anywhere?"

Looking at the beauty across the table, Bob considered he found Gerogina a rarity he valued highly, and nodded agreement.

Georgina excused herself while Bob took care of the bill. They carried the second bottle of wine with them.

"After all that wine, I think you'd better drive carefully." Georgina said.

"Don't worry. I won't speed through Jamaica Beach. They make too much money on traffic fines. This has been a pleasant evening even if we were talking about murder."

When Bob reached Georgina's home in Lafitte's Cove, she asked him in for coffee. "We must go in the front way. My garage opener is in the house."

Bob was happy to put his arm around her and help her up the steps. Inside, Georgina led him to the kitchen and began brewing coffee. "Sit down at the table while we wait. We'll take the coffee into my sitting room when it's ready."

Bob sat and looked about the kitchen. It had a dining area with a round table. On one side a counter extended to a stove top and oven. Cabinets lined the walls above the counter and stove. On the other side were more cabinets and a refrigerator-freezer. "Do you mind if I call you Georgie?"

"No, I'll be happy to be your Georgie girl," she laughed.

Georgina took off her jacket and put the wine bottle, coffee, and cookies on a tray. "You asked me where to find a live Eskimo curlew. I don't think you can. You'd have to make one," Georgina said.

"I reckon we'll have to wait for the Smithsonian to identify what was in that cage. We should have their report soon."

Georgina filled their cups with coffee and put it on the tray to take to the next room; she added sweetener and a dish with Brie and crackers. Then she picked up the tray and led the way to a coffee table in front of the sofa in what she called her sitting room. After turning on some classical music and cutting off the overhead lights, she asked Bob to sit beside her on the sofa.

The soft strains of Mozart's Clarinet Concerto in A Major complemented Georgina's voice with what Bob thought a sexy background. "I've enjoyed your company," he said. "Talking about murder this evening was more fun than I had thought possible, and I've learned a lot about birders and curlews."

"I've enjoyed the evening too," Georgina said, "and I may have drunk a little too much wine. Excuse me. If you need to use a restroom, there's one down the hall to the left."

Bob availed himself of the opportunity and was sitting on the sofa eating Brie and crackers and drinking coffee when Georgina returned. "This is a very pleasant place," Bob said. "What is that sweet aroma? I think I've smelled it before."

Georgina sat next to Bob. "You must smell the jasmine. You noticed some in my office. I love nature and heading a non-profit, but that doesn't mean I can't have nice things. You're surprised because you'd only seen me in my field clothes before tonight."

Bob laughed. "I must admit you're a bit sexier in that outfit you have on now."

Georgina snuggled against him as she put Brie on a cracker. "You have to admit you like me in my field clothes, too, though you didn't think them very sexy."

Putting his arm around her, Bob insisted he found her ravishing in whatever she wore. He leaned over and kissed her. "I liked that," she said as she returned the favor. She kicked off her heels and poured some more wine.

"You seem to know a lot about nature, Bob. Why aren't you a member of Birds & Floats? You hang out with us a lot. I believe you're a closet naturalist."

"I used to be a hunter, but I've seen so much blood and killing in my work that hunting with a gun doesn't appeal to me any more. Apart from work, I hunt with a camera and binoculars now."

Their discussions went on through more coffee and Brie for several hours filled with numerous kisses. Finally, Georgina told Bob it was her bedtime. "I've had a wonderful evening, and I want to see you again soon. Maybe you could come over for supper one evening. What about Friday? Would you be free?

"As of now, yes, I have a seven to four shift, but police officers often are called to extra duty at the last minute. If you can deal with that, I'd love to come for a meal Friday. What time?"

"Say seven. I can fix some of the meal ahead of time, but I'll have to work until five. I'll think about how to get an Eskimo curlew," Georgina smiled and kissed him goodnight at the door.

Chapter Nine

Leaving the sunny daylight and entering the acrid atmosphere of the station, Bob knew from the cigar smoke that the Chief had come in before him. He called Georgina at her office after he had begun drinking his first cup of coffee. He was following up on their conversation the night before. "Have you any more ideas about where to find an Eskimo curlew?"

"Not only thought about it, but I've done a bit of research. Our Eskimo curlew has a close relative, the Eurasian little curlew. The winter range of the little curlew includes northern Australia. Does that give you any ideas?"

Bob leaned forward and laughed. "You know it does. Do they look alike?"

"Quite a bit. It would take only a little paint to change a little curlew into an Eskimo curlew replica."

Bob restrained a yell of triumph with great effort. "You're a genius. That helps explain the Australian connection. We'll see what the Smithsonian says. I'll bet they confirm our suspicion."

After ending his conversation with Georgina, Bob emptied his coffee cup and quickly poured himself another and sat down to wait for Steve. Moments later, he smelled fresh cigar smoke, and the source of the smell materialized in a cigar-puffing Jerold Henderson. "Good morning, Chief," Bob said with an extra emphasis on good.

"Why are you so cheerful? Have you made progress on the serial rapist or the Frank murder?"

"I think I've figured out Frank's scam. I have to admit, Georgina Clayton gave me the clue. Now, we have to wait for the Smithsonian people to confirm our theory."

Just then Steve walked in and Bob said, "Georgina and I think we've solved the Australian connection," Bob said.

"Are you kidding?" Steve asked.

"I kept asking Georgina where anyone could get an Eskimo curlew for a scam, and she answered the question. You could use a little curlew, its Eurasian relative. It would take just a little paint."

"But where would you find a little curlew?" Steve asked. as he eased into the chair at his desk.

"In northern Australia. They winter there, Georgina says."

"An Australian aborigine would know just how to trap one," Steve said.

"I think you boys have to wait for what the Smithsonian says," Chief Henderson said. "But it sounds like you're going to get confirmation." Blowing a perfect smoke ring, Henderson sauntered to his office. trailing fumes.

Bob and Steve looked at each other, laughed, and gave thumbs up as they waved smoke away.

Later in the day, as Steve and Bob were reviewing their progress, a call for them came in. Steve picked up the phone." He heard a voice he had already learned.

"Is this Bob?" Emden asked.

He was happy to hear her voice. "No, it's Steve,"

"This is Emden. I have some good news."

"I don't mind hearing good news."

"I've thought of a way of find more about the second body dumped on Birds &

Floats. I recall seeing soil on the cage you found at the Frank murder site. If you

bring me the cage, I'll take some soil from it and send it to an acquaintance of mine in Australia who identifies soil types. She may be able to tell us where the soil came from."

Steve smiled. *No need for Bob to have all the pleasant jobs.* "I'll bring the cage right over," he said, as he wrote a note to put on Bob's desk.

After checking at the reception desk at the medical examiner's, Steve lifted the bagged cage and hurried to Emden's office. She looked up and greeted him when he appeared in her doorway. "It's good to see you again, Steve."

"You've been busy with our case—thanks; we have some ideas that explain the Australian connection you've uncovered. I have the cage, Dr. Castro," Steve said, speaking on the assumption a thank-you couldn't be harmful, even for a woman who spent her time fondling dead bodies. He handed her the bagged cage.

Emden smiled. "Thank you for the compliment," she said as she took the bag. "Most of the men I deal with don't seem to care."

Steve was a good inch taller than Bob, and he towered over Emden's five-foot- two. "Where should we work with the cage?"

"Let's go to my lab. I'll take soil samples there."

As Emden scraped soil samples from the cage, she dropped them in plastic bags. In all, she managed to obtain five samples. "I'll send these to my friend in Australia by express air. We should have an answer in a week or two if some of the soil is from there."

"Could I take you to lunch?" Steve asked. "I know of a great seafood place near here."

"It wouldn't be Benno's, would it?"

"Yes, you've eaten there. I remember that wonderful evening."

"Benno's seems very popular with Galveston police."

"That's because the food's good," Steve said.

Emden grinned. "It has a great reputation. I usually eat here, but I can't resist an invitation to Benno's"

"Great, how long before you're free?"

"All I have to do is hang up my lab coat and wash my hands."

Outside, Emden suggested they take her car. "We probably shouldn't use your police car."

At Benno's. as they stood in line, Steve admired her purple blouse and black slacks. He couldn't get enough of the deep pools he saw in her dark brown eyes set in a face so pretty he imagined Rembrandt would have had difficulty matching it. What a waste it was for her to spend her time with cadavers, but he kept these thoughts to himself. He didn't want to ruin his tough-guy image completely. He'd already let her drive.

"It's a beautiful day. Let's sit outside to get a view of the Gulf," Emden suggested, as she entered her order of Cajun oysters and lemonade. Steve also ordered Cajun oysters, but added a draft of beer. They took their number and their drinks outside and found a table.

"How is the case progressing?"

"Pretty well. Bob and Georgina Clayton think they've figured out the reason for the Australian connection. They think it involves the little curlew. It's a cousin of the Eskimo curlew, and it winters in northern Australia."

"I hope my colleague in Australia can pin down the location."

"Australia is a place I'd like to go one day."

"It sounds exciting," Emden said. "I met my Aussie colleague at a professional conference. Her descriptions were fascinating. I'd love to see a platypus."

Steve grinned. "So would I. They're look like ducks with fur, and I'd like to see some kangaroos in the wild."

Emden's face grew serious "For the time being I'll have to watch Australian animals on TV and in the Houston zoo." She sighed. "I have to pay back my debts for education. I had some scholarships, but it takes time and money to do graduate work, and I wanted a Ph. D."

"Why did you decide to become a pathologist?"

"I wanted to be an MD, but I can't stand the thought of cutting on a live person. On the other hand, I've never had a moment's problem dissecting a corpse. It wasn't a hard decision." Emden put her hand on his and laughed. "My patients never complain."

Too bad they can't admire your beauty. Afraid he might speak the thought, Steve pointed to the sky, "Look, that flock of pelicans is wheeling around to take a second look at us. So are the gulls."

"You're joking. The gulls just want our food. I hope they don't poop on us."

Steve reared back and down as if in terror. "As I recall, you wanted to sit out here."

Emden laughed. "You're a clown."

"This clown would like a date. It's a warm, clear day. I'll bet the beach would be great tonight."

"I love the beach at night."

"The beach at Galveston Island State Park's a great place. Where can I pick you up?"

"You can pick me up at my office again after six. I keep my bathing suit here so that I can take a dip after work. Should I wear my bathing suit under my clothes?"

"It's warm enough. Maybe just bring it and a towel. There're places to change at the beach, and you don't want to ride back in a wet suit if the evening's cool. You can suit yourself," Steve said, laughing at his pun with a nervous twitch of his head. He was looking forward to seeing Emden in a bathing suit.

When Emden dropped Steve off at his car, she told him she'd send the soil samples out right away. "I'll be ready at six," she said. "I'm glad I keep my bathing suit here."

ℤ ℤ ℤ

On the way back to the station, Steve stopped by his apartment and picked up a couple of towels, his swimsuit, and a kite. He put them in his truck and added a battery-powered CD player and CD's. He locked the truck and drove his police car back to the station. He planned to stop later for some food after he picked up Emden.

At the station, Steve apologized to Bob about his leaving just a note about taking the cage to Emden, "The cage is back in the evidence room. Emden says she might have an answer in a couple of weeks."

Bob grunted and poured himself another cup of coffee. "We're learning about the scam, but we still have a way to go with finding the murderers. We need to identify the owners of those other two sets of fingerprints."

"Okay, do you have a suggestion."

"I've had John send them to the FBI to enter them in their Automated Fingerprint Identification System. Maybe one of them belongs to somebody in their database."

Chapter Ten

After picking up Emden, Steve drove his truck west to Galveston Island State Park along the Seawall lit by a sun low in the sky an hour from sunset. Steve and Emden had to fight the glare with sunglasses. A three-quarters moon hung in the sky, waiting to light the night. Listening to a medley of John Denver music, Steve heard Emden humming *Annie's Song.*

"You remember John Denver?"

Emden laughed. "You must think I'm very young, but I remember when he died in the 90's. He didn't know enough about his new plane. I love his music. You don't find many people becoming Ph.D.'s in their teens, even the prodigies."

"You look young enough to be a teenager," Steve said as he eased the truck into the parking lot across from the beach entrance. "We can change in the restrooms. While you're changing, I'll carry things down to the beach. Do you like to fly kites?"

"I haven't done that for years, but I remember. It's fun."

"Let's try it out after you change, then." Later, as the kite rose in the sky and tugged at its string as it rose gracefully, Emden screamed in delight when Steve put the control in her hand. and left to change into his bathing suit.

When he reappeared, he took the kite from Emden. "We're lucky to have a good breeze," he said. "I'll fly it awhile."

Later, as he admired Emden's figure displayed well in her tight two-piece swim suit, he gave the cord back to her.

"You've put it up really high," she said as she controlled the kite.

After almost fifteen minutes, Emden tired and gave control of the kite back to Steve, who played with it another ten minutes before bringing the kite in and placing his boom box over it to keep it from blowing away.

As he looked around, he saw Emden had ventured into the water up to her waist. She had put on a plastic cap to protect her hair as she immersed herself in the Gulf and rode the next wave to the beach, where she landed at Steve's feet. He grabbed her hands and pulled her up, then wrapped his arms around her waist and pulled her face up to his lips and kissed her.

"Oh," she said, "I'll repeat that."

"The kiss?"

"No, silly, riding in on a wave to the beach," she said, laughing as she returned to the water. After savoring the kiss a moment, Steve followed her. Reaching her, he watched as she avoided his hand and rode another wave to the beach. Following, he picked her up and gently tossed her back into the Gulf. She went out and rode another wave in. As she splashed, and stood up, he caught her and kissed her again. She tried to pull away, but he picked her up and carried her back to their beach blanket and set her down. He handed her a towel. As they began drying, the last rays of the sun warmed them.

Sitting down beside her he opened the bag with their food, "It's time to eat," he said, handing her the thermos in which he'd kept warm tea to go with her grilled chicken and his burger and two orders of fries. He also had a bag of oatmeal raisin cookies stowed there. As they sat eating, Steve couldn't help noticing how becomingly her bathing suit clung to her body. "Do you exercise?" he asked.

"I do yoga in the morning and try to jog or walk in the evening."

"The exercise certainly seems to agree with you."

"Changing the subject, I remember what I found this afternoon examining the Australian's body."

"What's that?"

"Looking more carefully I noticed a number of small scratches on his arms and neck. I think he struggled with somebody, probably a woman with long fingernails. I took some fingerprints and samples of skin from around the scratches."

"What do you plan to do with them?"

"I've sent some skin samples off for analysis. Maybe we'll get enough information to identify the owner of another set of fingerprints. Whoever made the wounds left some blood. I may even be able to identify a blood type. I recovered some partial fingerprints. I'll make copies for you and Bob."

When they finished their burgers, fries, and cookies, Steve disposed of the trash in a nearby bin. Then he pulled out the kite and launched it again. "Let's work off the food flying the kite and then take another dip in the ocean."

Emden jumped up. "Get it up high and let me fly it."

They spent the last hour of evening light flying the kite. Then, by moonlight, Steve pulled it in, placing it back under the boom box. Together they reentered the Gulf. Going out to her waist again, Emden stopped. Steve went a bit farther and called to Emden. "Come on out; I'll take your hand." She went out until she could catch his stretched-out arm. He pulled her to him. They spent moments watching the waves roll in to shore in the moonlight. Then they picked a large wave and rode it back to the beach and waded back to wait for another.

Finally, after they had ridden several more waves, Steve lifted her up to his shoulders. Giggling, she pulled his ears. "The view up here is great, and the ocean breeze feels good. I love the smell of the ocean," she said. Carrying her, he walked back to the beach before putting her down on their beach towel.

Drying each other again before walking back to the edge of the water, they watched the waves thrust onto the sand, spreading foam over more dry sand with each big wave as the incoming tide wet more and more sand. "I love to watch the water wetting dry sand in the moonlight," Emden said.

Steve nodded. "The tide's coming in. It's fun to watch moonlight on the water wetting dry beach Look at that fiddler crab running across the sand away from the water."

Emden sighed. "I think the moonlight's romantic."

Steve pulled her to him and kissed her forehead. "I think it's romantic too. Your being here makes it romantic." He pulled her back down to the beach towel and turned on the music from the CD playing a medley of music from Broadway shows. For a long time they lay there and listened and watched as the tide kept wetting the beach closer and closer to them. Steve kissed her as she snuggled against him. For a long time they warmed each other. She made no protest as he invaded her suit's top and ran his hand over her breasts.

As he bent and kissed each breast, she sighed and ran her fingers through his hair. Holding her close, he picked her up walked back to the water until she could splash her toes in the Gulf. She snuggled against him. After a few minutes, he turned and walked back to the beach towel, eased her down and lay down beside her.

As the moonlight grew brighter, Steve kissed her breasts again and reached lower to her swim trunks. Emden denied him. "Stop." He knew she could detect his arousal. There was a brief silence. "You've already gone further than I should have let you." she said. "It felt good. I really like you, but I'm not into casual sex. If you care for me, you'll stop."

"I do care for you. I'm not about to rape you, but you can tell I need a time out."

"I'm not easy. It's my fault as much as yours. I was enjoying you. I didn't want to stop either." As they listened to the music on the CD, they held hands as Frank Sinatra sang, "The moonlight becomes you, it goes with your hair/You certainly know the right thing to wear…." Emden laughed at the irony. "It's a good thing I had on tight swim trunks."

"Where do you want to go on our next date?" he asked, as he caressed her.

Emden recalled their earlier conversation. "I think the Houston zoo would be a great place. I don't know if they have a platypus, but I'm sure they have kangaroos. You can pick me up at my home in Pasadena and meet my parents. You'll like my mother's cooking, and my father is as old-fashioned as you are."

₧ ₧ ₧

At the station the next morning, Steve told Bob what Emden had found on their new corpse. "'The Australian' had some scratches. It may turn out to be a means of identifying one of the killers. Emden has given me fingerprints that may give us a match."

"Good," Bob said. "I'll give these to John."

"I hope he can find something helpful."

"We're making great progress in uncovering the scam that led to the killings," Bob said, "but so far we haven't made much progress in finding the killers. At least the serial rapist has not done any rapes lately. Maybe he's gone elsewhere."

Steve nodded. "Maybe we'll hear from the Smithsonian or the FBI

soon. In the larger scheme of things, the murderers should be given medals for ridding us of anti-social crooks."

Bob shook his head, "Don't forget it's not our job to determine right or wrong. We're supposed to uphold the law. That means treating crooks with as much restraint as law-abiding people."

"And that other confederate who's not a murderer but is guilty of aiding and abetting?"

"I wonder how our flyer project with Georgina is progressing. I'll find out Friday night. She's cooking dinner for me."

"Sounds like you're getting serious."

"I don't plan to stay a bachelor all my life. Georgina's everything I've desired. The question is whether or not I'm what she desires."

"Well, stay away from Emden. I'm going to take her to the Houston zoo and meet her parents."

"I see a coon that's about trapped. That's serious. When did all that happen?"

"It came along like a hurricane. I just happened to be in the way. I'm having a hard time keeping my mind on hunting crooks."

Chapter Eleven

....

At seven o'clock Friday night, wearing a coat and tie, Bob rang the doorbell at Georgina's house in Lafitte's Cove. The woman who greeted him wore an aubergine blouse divided down the middle almost to the waist and a split scarlet skirt revealing her leg past the knees. Her hair was swept back in a pony tail floating over her bare back. Bob admired. "You look like a hostess expecting a special guest." When he detected a rich, savory smell, Bob asked, "What's that perfume? It seems familiar."

"That's fresh jasmine. You've smelled it before, remember?

'Yes. It turns me on."

"I've been expecting a special guest, my leader in solving crimes. Come in and kiss your special hostess," she said as she offered her lips. Bob kissed her and followed her in.

Georgina ushered him to her dining room table, where there were candles burning. "Sit down. I've poured you some wine, the wine we brought from Nate's. I'll have supper on the table in a jiffy." From the kitchen, she brought two plates, one for him with steak, rice, and asparagus and the other for her with salmon, rice, and asparagus. She lit two more candles on the table and switched off the overhead lights.

"I guessed you like your steak medium rare. If it isn't done enough, I can cook it a bit more."

Bob took a bite. "Medium rare is fine."

"Would you mind if we talk about our murders?" Georgina asked.

"Not at all." As they ate, Bob told her about the new information pointing directly to the use of a little curlew trapped in Australia, and the possibility that Emden had uncovered some information leading to the identity of one of the murderers. "We're waiting for the Smithsonian to confirm the identify of the feathers we found in the cage. Emden has found some partial prints for John Withers to check."

"I'm glad to hear about our progress," Georgina said as she gazed at Bob in the candlelight. He thought he saw an extra intensity in her face.

"Have you made any progress with the flyers?"

"We've distributed them to all of our members and employees, and we've been getting a lot back. Our rate of return is phenomenal. So far we've had some people say they have seen him but don't know his name. I have the returns safely tucked away here. You can take them and give them to your man to compare with the list I gave you. They were mailed to me here or given to me at work."

"Good, I couldn't ask for a better assistant." Bob saw that these words brought a smile to Georgina's face.

For dessert, Georgina served apple cobbler with vanilla ice cream topped in chocolate syrup. Bob praised her dinner, and she bragged she fixed the whole dinner herself. "I wanted you to know I'm not just a CEO of a non-profit."

"Whatever you do, I consider you a *nonpareil*. You're an amazing person."

They carried their wine glasses to her sitting room. She brought the wine bottle along too. She put the bottle on the coffee table. "Make yourself comfortable while I brew some coffee for us to have when the wine runs out."

"Take your time," Bob said as he refilled their wine glasses before heading for the john. He returned before his hostess brought in the coffee. He sat down and sipped his wine as he listened to Mozart's *The Marriage of Figaro* and looked at the Audubon prints Georgina had lining her walls.

When she brought in a tray with coffee cups, Brie and crackers, she put them on the coffee table next to the wine bottle. "I don't think the wine will last much longer," she said as she sat down beside Bob and snuggled up. "When the wine's gone, if the coffee's not enough, I'll fix some tea. I hope you like Mozart. His music pleases me."

"He's my favorite in the classical repertoire. You and I do have a lot in common."

"Yes, it's amazing how compatible we are. You're a reader of poets, you love nature, and you have shared your life with me. How could I ask for more?" She gave a toss of her head and laughed, then picked up some flowers she had cut earlier from a jasmine bush. She put them in a vase she placed on a small table near the sofa where Bob was sitting.

In the next half hour, they had finished the wine and begun the coffee, so Georgina fixed the tea she had promised.

"I like the way you decorated your home," Bob said as strains of *Don Giovanni* spread through the room along with the scent of jasmine, which grew stronger as Georgina sat beside him. She untied Bob's tie and hung it over the back of the sofa. "If you take off your jacket, I'll get out of these heels and let down my hair."

Bob was quick to oblige. Taking off his jacket, he raised an almost empty glass of wine and offered a toast. "Here's to our having become well acquainted." Putting his wine down, he turned and kissed her long and deep while running his hand along her leg to the split of her skirt. Georgina kept her part of their bargain.

Comfortable, she pulled his hand away from her leg and placed it upon the split of her blouse between her breasts where she had placed a jasmine blossom. "If you'll unzip this skirt, I'll slip out of it," Georgina said as she guided his other hand to the zipper."

As he pulled the zipper down, she stepped out of the skirt and removed her blouse. Like Botticelli's Venus rising from the sea, she had nothing on beneath. Bob gazed at her nakedness, awestruck by its beauty.

"Do you like what you see, Detective?" she asked as she pulled him from the sofa. He nodded as she reached for her coffee and drank, "Here's to our getting acquainted even better," she said as she raised her cup.

Putting her drink down, she unbuttoned his shirt and unbuckled his pants. "Off with those clothes, Sweetheart." He voiced no objection. She kissed him and stood, waiting for him to complete disrobing. "Please— join me in nakedness," she said as she kissed his cheek. He fulfilled her plea as quickly as he could, then stood next to her, feeling lucky he had not acquired excess fat, but a bit nervous. He hid his partial erection beneath his hand as she positioned her cell phone to take a selfie of them.

He voiced a question. "Are you a nudist?"

"No, I'm not a nudist," Georgina said. "Don't be nervous. I just wanted to see you and for you to see me, because I plan to marry you—if that's all right with you." She proceeded to rub him with jasmine oil.

Startled, Bob searched for speech. "I…ah…think … ah…this marriage proposal is sudden and unusual, uh… ah…but I accept." He couldn't have chosen better himself. He was glad they were so compatible, but he recalled John Milton's Adam, *fondly overcome by female charm* when Eve tempted him to eat the forbidden apple. In a few moments he decided the analogy was false.

"This ceremony smacks of entrapment, but I'm enjoying my captivity," he said, as she raised her phone to take another selfie of them.

Smiling, Georgina put her arms around his neck and kissed him. "Now my proposal and your acceptance are on record. If we were in Elizabethan England, we would be considered married now, but I have a tape of our vows, and we can have a more formal ceremony any time you please. Now, follow me." She led him into the master bedroom, bringing the vase of jasmine flowers, "Here's our marriage bed, Honey. I hope you like it."

A bit overwhelmed still, but beginning to get his bearings, he nodded. "I'm looking forward to using it."

"How does it feel to be a married man?" she asked as she nibbled his ear.

Finally in control, Bob grinned. "I'll tell you in the morning. I won't feel married until the marriage is consummated."

"I said a prayer for a good performance," she said. "I want you to show my prayer has been answered."

"I'll do my best to answer your prayer." Bob said as he lowered her to their marriage bed.

When he awoke at six in the morning, Bob felt very tired but very happy. He shook his new wife awake. She yawned and asked, "What do you want, Sweetheart?"

"I want to know whether my performance was satisfactory. I tried to make it memorable. I wanted to make sure I answered your prayer."

Georgina laughed and kissed him. "Beyond satisfactory. Just thinking about it makes me lustful."

After Bob had quenched her desire, they had a quick breakfast of cereal and coffee, and Bob put on his clothes they had hung up the night before. He made it to work on time. At the station, Bob poured himself a cup of coffee and sat at his desk. He tried to review the Frank case, but he kept thinking of his wedding night. It was not like he had envisioned his marriage would be, but much better. He hoped he could continue to please Georgina. She pleased him. He was certain about that. She was all that he had ever dreamed of—and much more.

Steve came in a few minutes later and sniffed the air. "Instead of cigar smoke, this station smells more like a florist's shop."

"A great improvement, I think," Bob said.

After more joking, they reviewed the Frank case until John Withers came in with a message from the Smithsonian. "Good news, the Smithsonian confirms your belief that a little curlew was in the cage. They also say somebody had painted the curlew—beyond doubt to resemble an Eskimo curlew."

Bob had mixed emotions of triumph and frustration. "We have the scam figured out, but now we have to find the killers."

Steve nodded. "That may be tough. Emden might help us with her analysis of those samples she took from our second victim,""

"I'll bet that little curlew escaped," Bob said, laughing. "I wonder how many people will report seeing an Eskimo curlew on the island in the next few weeks? Not many will be sharp enough to identify a little curlew painted to resemble an Eskimo curlew."

"We need to get Emden and Georgina on the payroll."

Chapter Twelve

During the afternoon, Steve received a call from Emden. "I have more samples of fingerprints that I've taken from our Australian corpse. Why don't you come over and pick up a copy to compare with your mystery prints?"

"Emden has some evidence. She found more fingerprints on our Aussie." Steve volunteered, "I'll go over and pick up the prints now. She has them ready."

Laughing at Steve's eagerness, Bob agreed to a more boring but needed chore, "Okay. I'll help John with the flyers." Bob knew John could use some help. Georgina had given him more returned flyers that morning. He had added them to John's large pile.

Steve found Emden in her office. She stood and greeted him, poured two cups of coffee, and handed one to him. "Make yourself comfortable," she said as she gave him a plastic bag with a copy of the fingerprints. These should match some you already have, unless still another person is involved in the murders."

Steve scratched his brow. "We could use a break. We've been gaining a fairly good idea about the scam, but we don't know what prompted the collapse of the scheme and the murders."

Emden pointed to a picture on her wallboard that Steve recognized as the Australian victim. "I discovered his name. Meet Jameson Kanger. Maybe the name will help."

"It gives us a starting point. Have you heard anything about the soil you sent off?"

"I have a preliminary answer. It's from a part of the little curlew's winter range. So our dead guys could have found one there."

"Are we still on for the Houston zoo this Sunday?" Steve's voice seemed to him to be a little too anxious.

"Unless you receive special duty. You should come to my home around eleven-thirty. You can meet my parents and have Sunday dinner with us."

"Okay, I still have the address you gave me." She walked to her door with him, and he kissed her before he turned to leave. "Do you think your parents will approve of me?"

"I'm a liberated woman. I don't need their approval." She smiled. "I'm sure they'll like you," she added with a laugh. "You and my dad are a lot alike. It took him a long time to adjust to my working with corpses."

≔ ≔ ≔

Tired of looking at flyers, Bob could not resist calling Georgina before his workday was over.

"I'll have news for you tonight."

"I have news for you too. Do you like barbecue?"

"Sure, I love it."

"Then please drop by Queen's and pick up two Slider Specials for supper. I want pork with barbequed beans and slaw. I won't waste time cooking.

Daydreaming, Bob almost forgot to tell her Withers was having good luck matching the flyers with the members list.

"I think you should try to find out how many of your members have Australian connections. We may find some among the people who don't return the flyers."

Bob's work on the flyers was interrupted again later by the return of Steve with the fingerprints. Steve and Bob compared them with what they had been calling their mystery prints. They thought they might have a match. "We could tell better if we had a thumb print, Steve said.

"I reckon we'd better have John check these out," Bob said. "He

needs a break from working with the flyers."

Bob walked down the hall past Chief Henderson's office. He could tell by the smell of cigar smoke that the Chief was in. Down farther he found John Withers taking a break from flyers by throwing darts at a dartboard decorated with Al Capone's picture on the wall.

Interrupted in mid throw, Withers griped. "I was just about to hit Al in the eye."

"John, I know you need a break from the flyers. Steve and I have been comparing prints Emden Castro has taken off the Australian with those we call the mystery prints. Unfortunately there's no thumbprint. We'd like your opinion."

Withers put down the darts he was holding. "I believe I could use a break. I'm tired of looking at Capone's picture and the Aussie's. Let me have the prints."

"We've got a name now, Emden discovered the Aussie's name, Jameson Kanger."

⁚   ⁚   ⁚

Looking at the face on the flyer, Margaret Smith rubbed her eyes before taking a second look. It wasn't her imagination. The picture was of Jameson Kanger, apparently no longer alive. Maggie thought about birding with Aussie Bird Tours. Kanger had been a competent co-leader on the northern section of the trip, but he had raped Patsy. He and Porky were planning a nefarious scheme of some kind. She couldn't summon up any sorrow for Jameson's demise. He and Porky had vied in showering her with their time and birding knowledge. In the process, the two men got to know each other fairly well, each learning the other's dark side, Maggie guessed.

She and Jameson had hit it off at first. Maggie was enjoying her return to her native land as a birder, and she had appreciated the special attention Jameson gave her in identifying birds until he and Porky had begun hatching their scheme, whatever it was. She was not surprised to learn of Jameson's death—undoubtedly well deserved. After he raped Patsy, they had kept as far from him as possible.

Now Maggie had this flyer to deal with. She resolved to ignore it, because Porky had asked her not to say anything about seeing him in Galveston. He had spent a few nights with her in her two-story home in the conservation district when he arrived unannounced. He had made love to her again and promised, "I'll want to spend all of my time with you when I finish my current project."

Maggie had raised an eyebrow. "Why should I believe you? How do you know I want you around?"

To reassure her, Porky had left her his traveling bag and two thousand dollars to keep quiet at Birds & Floats about seeing him. Skeptical, she had searched the suitcase and found another ten thousand dollars hidden there. She thought she'd better ignore the flyer. She didn't want to lose Porky, no matter his being a crook, and she didn't want to admit she knew Jameson Kanger. Maggie felt she ought to consider what to do. Maybe she should talk to Patsy before doing anything.

She wouldn't betray Porky, although she hadn't heard from him again after he left for the meeting with Mackensie Craft she'd arranged. If he were still alive, she didn't want to lose him. Patsy would have received one of these flyers too. She needed to see Patsy and talk things over. Aware she didn't need to make an immediate decision, Maggie opened a desk drawer and dropped the flyer in. Next, she moved Porky's suitcase to a hiding place in a closet. Then she called Patsy.

Receiving no answer, she went outside to cut some flowers and greenery for a floral arrangement. She found gladiolus, roses, and zinnias to go with some green papyrus and branches of a butterfly bush. She cut enough jasmine to add to the aroma of her indoor potted plant. By the time Patsy returned her call, Maggie had created what she thought splendid arrangements for her mantelpiece and bedroom.

"Hello, Maggie. I'm sorry I missed your call. What's on your mind?"

"Patsy, did you get one of the flyers with Jameson's photo on it?"

"I sure did. I'm glad the son of a bitch got what was coming to him. I can't say I'm sorry, even though I'm probably carrying his child."

"I haven't heard from Porky for weeks. Do you know anything about him?"

"He's dead, too. It's a big mess. I don't want to talk about it on the phone. I'll come over and tell you what I know."

≔ ≔ ≔

At the what had become his home, Bob tried the door before pulling out the key Georgina had given him. The door was open. As he entered with the barbecue and closed the door, the scent of jasmine struck him. Georgina emerged from the master bedroom in a loose chemise extending a foot above her knees.

After they finished their barbecue dinner, Georgina fixed margaritas. She handed him a glass and held hers in one hand while she sat on his lap facing him. As they sipped their drinks, she ran her hands over his chest. "How does that feel, Honey?"

"Very soothing."

"Good. I want you to relax. But we almost forgot the murders."

Bob muttered. "How could we? The Australian's name is Jameson Kanger."

Georgina. sighed. "I don't care for that name, but. I've learned Margaret Smith knew a Porky. I'll bet she's involved in the murders somehow."

Chapter Thirteen

When a tired Robert Bruce dragged into the Galveston police station the next morning, he found John Withers again throwing darts at the board emblazoned with Al Capone's likeness. John retrieved his dart and greeted Bob with a grin. "It's almost certain that the prints you gave me match one of those found on the shotgun used to shoot Frank. I believe they belong to a woman."

"Great work. Georgina gave me some more flyers to bring in, so I reckon we have to work with them. They've come in faster than expected, so we'll be able to start on the no-shows right away. We could skip the ones that have come in and just deal with people on our list of Boats & Floats people who've been to Australia in the last three months. The sooner we get these done, the sooner we can find the confederate who isn't guilty of murder—probably just obstruction of justice if the flyer isn't in—and maybe a killer."

Bob turned to Steve, who had just arrived. "You help John with the flyers for a while. I'm going to take that list Georgina gave us and check the traveling those on the list have done lately. We need to know if any of them have been to Australia. I'll go up to Bush and check."

Steve made no objection to taking on a boring task. Bob wasn't surprised that Steve didn't object. He wasn't looking forward to the hectic, unpleasant drive on I-45 to Bush International Airport. He might enlist Georgina to go with him, since she took such pleasure in the case. It wouldn't hurt to call.

"Georgie, could you spare the time to find flights to Australia among your members and go with me to Bush International to check on the travel of people on the list you gave me? I think we might turn up somebody who's been to Australia in the last few months."

"I don't have any appointments, Bobby. I'll help compile a list of Australian flights, and I'd love to go with you, if you give me time to change from my field clothes."

"Okay, I'll come by your office, and we can use your computers to check the flights. I don't think that should take us too long. If we don't finish making the list today, could you go tomorrow?

"Yes, but it shouldn't take us long to do the list of flights. I could check Australian lines while you check United, American, Continental and Delta. Then we can do any others together," Georgina said.

They had their information well before noon.

"We can go today," Bob said. "You go change, and I'll pick you up at your place, or should I say our place, in an hour." Reminded that he still hadn't released his apartment, he called the rental agent to say he was giving up his lease at the end of the month. He thought of all the other changes he had to make, but he had no complaints. Living with Georgie was too delightful. Life with her was pure pleasure. He still looked back at her method of proposal with amazement, amusement, and wonder at how he could be so lucky.

Georgina stood on the porch waiting when Bob arrived, a little late. Again, he saw her transformed. This time to a very professional woman in a gray zip pocket pants suit with a white-buttoned gray jacket with a black blouse underneath. "Do I look like a detective in this outfit?"

Appraising her outfit and the way she filled it, he nodded. "But you look good to me in anything, and even better in nothing." She leaned over and kissed him.

"You're a romantic."

"You've been clipping jasmine. It'll be hard to keep my mind on driving," he said. "You're a big teaser."

"I have to keep your interest," Georgina looked at herself in the mirror on the sun shield. "I'll put on some lipstick before we get to the airport."

After a drive through heavy traffic on Interstate 45, Bob took the exit to the airport and parked in the short-term lot. The two of them walked across the covered roadway. They dodged traffic and breathed unpleasant fumes. After enduring bus and auto traffic, they entered the section for departures. Bob showed his identification and asked to see someone who could help them.

They were directed to an office where several women were working with computers. Bob showed his ID and handed one of them his list of names and explained they were working on murder cases involving Australia. "We need to know if any of the people on this list have made a trip to Australia in the last four months."

The woman introduced herself as Lois and looked over their list. She didn't seem to need the list of airlines they had created   She scanned their list of people into their system and scanned the names automatically into a computer. Then she requested the computer to furnish the names of any of these people who had been on a flight to or from Australia in the last four months. At Bob's request she checked flights into and out of Hobby as well as Bush International. In less than twenty minutes they had a list of these travelers.

Georgina professed amazement at the speed with which they got their answer, and Bob thanked Lois for her help. "Don't mention it," she said. "It's my pleasure to help the police."

As they walked to the car, Georgina asked how many names were on the list Lois had developed. "Fifteen," Bob said. "It shouldn't take us long to question any who haven't turned in flyers and cross check them with this list. I'm amazed. We wasted time compiling that list of flights. Two of the people on the list she gave us are dead: Hammond Frank and Jameson Kanger." He handed her the list. "See if you recognize any of the other names."

"I recognize several of them," Georgina said after a cursory inspection: Margaret Smith and Patricia Shaper. It will be easy to compare this list with our returned flyers. If there are any who haven't sent flyers, his wife back, you can start with them right away."

"Let's head back. We can stop someplace and have lunch, or would you rather go home for lunch?"

"I'm afraid if we go home, we'd never get back to work today. Let's stop for the lunch buffet at Mario's on 61st Street."

"Lots of variety, and we can get back to work in a hurry.

"I need go home after lunch. Drop me off. I can change back into my field clothes and drive to my office."

Back at the station, Bob showed Steve the list they had received at the airport. "Two of them are our murder victims. I added to the Boats & Floats list. That leaves just thirteen. We can compare this list with the list of unreturned flyers. If any on our short list haven't turned in a flyer, they're the ones we should begin questioning."

Making sure to keep the unexamined flyers and those already examined in different piles, they began to match names on the list from the airport with names on the unexamined flyers. It took the rest of the afternoon and a little longer. Bob let the other two go and finished the chore in another half an hour's work. By that time there were five names left unmatched plus one on the unreturned list who didn't match the airport list.

Realizing how late it was, Bob called Georgina to let her know he was coming home. "I know I'm late, but I wanted to get this job done. There are five names on the airport list not matched with flyers, plus one other. We'll start working on them tomorrow. What do you want to do for dinner?"

"I'm cooking dinner. I'll have it ready by the time you get home, if you're leaving now."

"I'm on my way out the station."

Bob paid little attention to the speed limit and arrived at Lafitte's in fifteen minutes. He locked the door behind him and watched as Georgina brought out their suppers, salmon for both. She had wine for her and a whiskey sour for him beside their water glasses. Wearing only the chemise she had worn the night before, she took off his jacket and gave him a hug and a long kiss. "I love you, Bobby. I think of you all the time."

Bob breathed in the jasmine scent radiating from her. "I can't get you out of my mind either. As John Denver sings, 'You fill up my senses.' I swear you do.'"

After dinner, he helped her clear the table. Then she led him to their bedroom and helped him undress. Later, as they listened to a Mozart clarinet concerto, Bob gave her the list of six unmatched names. All but one had Australian connections.

She immediately called his attention to Margaret Smith as a likely candidate for the person who might be an unwitting ally of Hammond Frank. "Margaret is an outgoing person who forms friendships with many people—even many other people consider misfits. Remember, I told you that somebody said she has mentioned a person named Porky."

Bob kissed Georgina. "Great, she's on our list of inter-viewees. Maybe this is the break we've needed."

Georgina put on some Mozart and took her time undressing Bob as he covered her with kisses and removed her chemise. They spent well into the night with a variety of love-making.

Chapter Fourteen:

Next morning Bob showed Steve the six finalists. Though Georgina had suggested starting with Margaret Smith, Steve was in favor of taking the names alphabetically. "It will raise less suspicions in the others," he said. "Five names on our list are of women."

Bob shrugged. He figured alphabetic order made as much sense as any, and he had his mind full of one woman, his wife. He didn't have much room for any more.

"Okay, you'll take the lead in questioning the first three and I'll take the last two."

Steve called Allison Black into the interrogation room. A Birds & Floats bag in hand, a tall young woman about five feet seven inches tall with brown hair and dark brown eyes came in. At first she did mot seem fazed by the dark walls, ceiling, and the two-way mirror of the interrogation room, but after looking around, she said it wasn't the coziest place she'd ever seen. "Who smokes the stinking cigars?" she asked as she sniffed the odors in the drab room.

John Withers appeared with equipment to take Allison's fingerprints. While he rolled her thumb onto the inkpad and then onto paper, Allison asked if something could be done about the cigar odor. As he completed the fingerprinting, Withers said "I'll be back with some air freshener."

As he ushered Allison to a chair, Steve appraised her figure and her unhappy face. "Why did you go to Australia, Miss Black?"

"I won a contest in which Boats & Floats had offered a grand prize of an all-paid trip to Australia. It was a wonderful trip. Why do you ask?"

Before Steve could answer, Withers entered the room and sprayed it with air freshener. "I hope that helps," he said as he left.

She was moving nervously in her chair, so Steve tried to put her at ease. Smiling, he said, "I hope that freshener improves our room, Miss Black. Did you know anybody in Australia before you went?" Steve asked.

"No. I didn't know a soul there. I just wanted to see a platypus."

"Did you see one?" Steve asked.

Allison turned head away from her questioner and popped a piece of gum in her mouth. Turning back, she smiled and said, "Sure did. Saw a family of three. They're strange-looking animals."

Steve grinned. "What kind of job do you have?" Steve asked, as he regarded her gum chewing with tolerance, pleased she was becoming relaxed.

He shifted in his seat, as he accepted the unpleasant sight confronting him.

Stopping her chewing, apparently sensing his distaste, she answered. "I'm a receptionist for a dentist right now, but I'm working on a certificate in medical office administration at Galveston College."

"Do you have relatives in Australia?

"No, I told you I didn't know anybody there. I may have some distant cousins there, but I don't know for sure. I entered a contest that had a trip to Australia as a prize because I wanted to see all of the strange animals and plants in the wild. I love nature. Besides, my great grandfather was one of the original white settlers."

"Weren't they all transported convicts?"

Allison's face crinkled with irritation. "Yes, but he was convicted of stealing a few loaves of bread so he could stay alive. He was a good man."

Feeling he wasn't getting anywhere, Steve pulled out a copy of the flyer with Kanger's photo. "Did you receive one of these flyers?"

Allison stopped chewing. "I remember seeing one in my mail. So what?"

Steve assumed a stern demeanor. "Why haven't you answered it and sent it back in the addressed envelope?"

Allison betrayed a hurt expression. "I'm a busy woman. Have you held down a full-time job and gone to college at the same time?"

"As a matter of fact, I have."

Allison smiled. "Then you know how it is. I just couldn't get around to filling it out." She reached over and put her hand on his. "You know how it is."

Steve recalled the hectic days when he did that very thing. He decided to end the interview. He paused and looked at Bob, who was grinning. Then Withers stuck his head in the door and said, "No match."

Steve decided retreat was his best option. "All right, Miss Black. Thank you for coming in. You may go."

Evidently relieved, Allison Black put her gum in a tissue, smiled, and handed Steve her business card. "If you're not too busy, give me a call sometime." She waved as she left the room.

"I didn't do that very well," Steve said.

Having overheard the interrogation, Bob could hardly contain laughter, but managed to get by with just a smirk.

"Look on the bright side. You've been asked for a date by a very pretty girl. I wonder what Sherill Cortes is like."

"I should have asked Allison if she knew a Hammond Frank or somebody going by the nickname of Porky."

Bob laughed. "Okay, so you did a lousy interview. She was pretty and obviously smitten with you."

Later that morning, Sherill Cortes came in. She was a plump, middle-aged woman with a wedding ring on her finger. Relieved by the age and appearance of his interviewee, Steve explained that they would take her fingerprints. After Withers had finished, Steve began his questioning. He felt easier asking questions of Sherill than he had of Allison. "Did you receive a flyer like this one?" He handed her a copy of the flyer.

"I didn't see it until yesterday. It was in the mail my husband collected while I was in Australia. I just got back."

"Did you happen to see the man in the picture?"

"No, I went to see my daughter and granddaughter. My daughter's husband was sent by his company to manage their branch in Australia."

"Did you meet somebody named Hammond Frank? Or someone using the nickname of Porky?"

"No, I'm sorry not to be of help."

Just then Withers stuck in his head and said, "No match."

Steve was disappointed but polite. "Thanks for coming in Ma'am."

As she went out the door, Steve looked over at Bob. "We don't seem to be making much progress."

"That's incorrect. You're doing routine police work. It's often boring, but it's necessary."

About four-thirty, Gretchen Fowler came in for questioning.

A short, handsome, slightly overweight bleached-blonde in her late thirties, she constantly twisted the ring on her finger, so Steve thought he might be interviewing somebody who would be of help. After Withers finished with the fingerprinting, Steve began.

"Did you receive a copy of this flyer?"

She nodded.

"Why haven't you sent it back?"

"I have to work. My husband's dead. I'm a busy woman."

"Why did you fly to Australia?"

"I've always wanted to see the strange land down under. My son is stationed there as part of an American military mission, so I thought this was my chance to see him, Australia, and some kangaroos at the same time. I've always loved nature and I've taught him to love it too."

"Did you meet somebody like the man in the picture on the flyer? Or somebody named Hammond Frank, or going by the nickname Porky?"

"Yes."

Steve perked up. "Could you tell me about your experience?"

"Certainly, I stood behind him and the guy whose picture was on the flyer in line while waiting for my flight home. The guy in the picture called the guy with him Porky. They both looked unwashed, and their clothes looked as if they'd been in a jungle. I was glad I didn't have to sit near them. They stunk. I won't forget them."

Steve tried to sound encouraging. "Did you hear them say anything else?"

"I heard the guy in the picture tell the Porky guy something would get there okay or all right."

"Can you remember anything else?"

"I don't recall, exactly, but I got the impression that the something was an animal of some kind . The Porky guy seemed to be very concerned about whatever it was."

"Did they say where they were headed?"

"I did hear the Porky guy mention Texas."

"When was your flight?"

"Four weeks ago this past Monday. I hope that I've helped. I can't recall anything else. I didn't see them again."

Withers interrupted, "No match."

Steve decided to end the questioning. "Mrs. Fowler, you've been a great help. Thank you."

Bob stood and told Steve he'd see Mrs. Fowler to the door. "We may need you again to testify," he told her." Those two men we asked about were murdered. Would you mind testifying, if our case comes to trial?"

"Murdered? No, no indeed. How exciting. They were both killed?"

"Yes. we're trying to find the killer."

"Right here in Galveston?'

"Yes. here on the island."

ⅎ   ⅎ   ⅎ

Bob called Georgina to tell her what Gretchen Fowler had said. "I've been thinking about Maggie Smith," Georgina said, "since her name came up. I think I did hear her mention a Porky several times. I've been so busy with my work and thinking about you that I didn't recall it well before today."

Bob slapped his thigh. "She's on our list for questioning tomorrow. This will be a big help. Do you want to go out for dinner tonight?"

"No, I'll cook something. I'm leaving work early. That's the nice thing about being boss of Birds & Floats. I can choose my own personal boss and match his schedule."

"By now, you've guessed I'd consult with you on almost any decision of importance." He wanted her to know how much he valued her help.

She laughed. "Then get ready to consult tonight. I have lots of good ideas about things for the boss to order."

Bob couldn't help wondering what her ideas were. Considering how she had proposed marriage, he would have to be ready for anything. He reckoned he might enjoy whatever her ideas were, though.

❧ ❧ ❧

The first light of morning was creeping through the pink bedroom drapes at Margaret Smith's. On the bedside table a brass figure of Priapus lay prone with large testicles and penis protruding upwards, a cherished memento of her life with Hank. Beside a two-headed dildo, Patsy Shaper lay naked, half asleep on Maggie's bed beside a naked Maggie, who was half awake.

Hearing the alarm, Patsy groaned. She had come to Maggie for comfort the night before, and they had spent almost all of the night talking about Kanger and Porky as they sought solace from each other. Patsy had told Maggie about Porky's death. "I haven't seen anything in the papers yet. The police must be trying to keep it secret."

Maggie nodded. "Porky was fun though he was a cad. He could make you laugh while he was robbing you. Have you made any decision about the abortion?"

Patsy cursed. "That motherfucker Jameson was another matter. The son of a bitch laughed when I told him I thought I was pregnant. The bastard offered to fuck me until I miscarried."

Maggie offered a solution. "You could abort. The sooner, the.better.

Porky left me a stash of cash. You could use it to pay for terminating the pregnancy."

"That's kind of you. I'll think about it. I've always been opposed to abortion, but that was before I needed one. Right now I've got to dress and go to the police station. They're interviewing the people who didn't turn in that flyer with Kanger's picture. I'll come by and tell you about it. You're on their list too, I suppose?"

"Yes, I'm scheduled for an interview this afternoon. I've been worrying about what to say."

"Before I go, I need to soothe my nerves. I'm afraid they'll catch me in a lie. But if I tell the truth, I'll be in *big* trouble. I need a drink."

Maggie handed her a pill and a glass of water. "Take this. It'll calm you."

"I hope it works."

"Tell the truth. You can plead self-defense. You didn't kill Kanger, did you?"

"No, but I had a motive."

"But you and I are the only ones who know that now. And Porky was an accident, wasn't he?"

"Yes, I was just trying to scare Mackensie Craft. He grabbed the shotgun, and I was trying to keep him from pulling it away."

"You can tell what happened, Honey." Maggie emphasized her point by hugging Patsy.

Patsy forgot her fear for a moment, but then she recalled the scene of the murder and shivered. "If I do, Mack might kill me," she said.

"You don't want to spend the rest of your life in jail, and I don't want to lose you. "

"You'd lose me for sure if Mack knifed me."

"You need to tell the truth."

The rising sun had cast its light upon the room, and Priapus was casting a shadow. "I'd better get to the police station, " Patsy said, pulling back the drapes and beginning to dress.

Maggie half-closed the drapes. "We should be careful. There might be a peeping tom."

Chapter Fifteen

In the morning, Bob Bruce woke from a dream in which he found himself swimming in warm ocean water while being nibbled by fish. As he gradually awakened, he began to understand his dream. The small fish gradually transformed into Georgie. "Wake up, Sleepyhead. I was enjoying watching you, but we have to go to work."

"That's right. Steve and I are interviewing an Olympic trap skeet champion this morning, Patricia Shaper. She's a prime suspect, an expert with shotguns. We'll take her fingerprints and see if they match a pair we found on the murder weapon. We may have one killer charged today. In the afternoon we see Margaret Smith."

Bob noticed his clothes fit a little looser now, as he dressed for work. He was losing weight from his nightly exertions and the exercise program Georgina had prescribed for him. The exercise had rid him of any excess fat. He needed to be alert to do the questioning, so the first thing he did after noting the Chief's cigar smoke was fix a cup of coffee.

As he was pouring coffee, Bob spoke to Steve. "I think we both should be questioning again today. I'll take the lead. These last two interviews will be most important. They might even solve the case."

Steve said he would try to do better with these suspects. "It's okay with me if you take the lead; I'll be the tough cop."

Both Bob and Steve were fully awake when Patricia Shaper arrived. After they introduced themselves, Bob ushered John Withers into the interrogation room. "Ms. Shaper, unless you object, we are going to begin by taking your fingerprints. Officer Withers will instruct you through the process." Patsy remained silent throughout the fingerprinting, promptly doing what Withers asked. As soon as Withers left with her prints, Bob asked her to sit down at the table. He and Steve sat across from her.

"Did you recently receive a flyer from Birds & Floats with a picture of a man on it?" asked Bob.

"Yes."

"Why haven't you returned it?"

"I get a lot of mail. I haven't answered half of what was waiting for me when I came home from my trip to Australia. The flyer was near the bottom of the pile."

Bob picked up a new copy of the flyer and shoved it in front of Patricia. "Do you recognize this man?" Shaper held the flyer up and examined it at length. Playing his role, Steve pretended irritation. "Do you or do you not, know the person in the picture, Ms. Shaper?"

She squirmed in her chair, looking up at the ceiling. "Uh…I think he was one of our tour leaders in northern Australia."

"What is his name?" Bob asked.

"We knew him as Jameson Kanger."

"How well did you know Kanger?"

"Well, everyone on a birding tour relies on the leaders to identify plants, birds and other animals."

"What about after tour hours? Did you socialize with him?"

"Sometimes groups would hang around and talk after dinner."

At this point John Withers opened the door and asked to see Bob in the hall. "We have a match with one set of prints on the shotgun," he said when he closed the door.

Back at the table, Bob asked, "Do you own a shotgun, Ms. Shaper?"

Shaper's face expressed indignation, Bob thought. "Of course I do, I'm an Olympic champion in Women's Trap Skeet. I'm an expert with a shotgun. I keep several shotguns at my home. Guns for my Olympic and world championship competitions and one for home defense,"

"Do you own a double-barreled shotgun?"

"Yes, it's home in my gun rack," she said.

"Would you be surprised if I told you we have a double-barreled shotgun with your fingerprints on it found at a murder scene?"

Patricia Shaper rose from her chair. "It's not my shotgun," she said. "I won't answer anymore questions now. I want counsel before I answer more questions." Her nervous stomach made noise.

"That's your choice," said Steve, but I'm arresting you for the murder of Hammond Frank." Steve stepped outside and called an officer. "Take her to booking and book her for murder. She's asked for a lawyer. See that she gets her phone call."

⅚ ⅚ ⅚

Maggie kept waiting to hear from Patsy, but no word came. She spent the rest of the morning wondering. Finally, she called the police station and asked if Patricia Shaper had left.

"Who is this?" said an officer.

"A friend. She promised to call me."

"Ms. Shaper will not be leaving jail in the immediate future."

Maggie assumed Patsy had used her phone call to get an attorney. She was worried but figured she'd better spend her time preparing for her own interview in the afternoon. She said to herself she had given Patsy good advice: tell the truth; just don't volunteer anything. If Maggie kept quiet about the rape, Patsy would be all right. She couldn't do anything for Porky, but she could protect Patsy. She suspected the murderer must be Mackensie Craft or Mack the Knife as he was often called by people familiar with *The Three-penny Opera*. Porky was still alive when Patsy had run away from Craft. The safest course for her friend, Maggie decided, was not to mention Mackensie unless asked specifically about him.

That afternoon Maggie arrived for her interview five minutes early. She was ushered into the drab interrogation room. Again, the first order of business was to fingerprint her before questioning. She complied, but gradually became agitated. "I dislike the tobacco odor in here. I'm allergic to cigars. Can't you do something about the odor? I'll get sick if I stay cooped up with that smell," Maggie protested.

Withers left and returned quickly with some air freshener. "We keep this around for just this purpose," John said. He sprayed the room with a pine-scented spray until the cigar smell could not be detected. That problem solved, Withers completed the fingerprinting and left.

When they returned to the questioning, Bob asked Margaret Smith if they might proceed; and she agreed that she felt much better.

"I'm sorry to have caused trouble, Detective."

"No problem, we appreciate your cooperation," Bob said. He didn't think this well-preserved woman in her early thirties was a killer, but she could be the unwitting confederate they had suspected to be a part of their puzzle.

"Why haven't you returned this flyer from Birds & Floats?" Steve asked. as he shoved a copy of the flyer with Jameson's picture in front of her.

Maggie shifted in her chair. "I have a pile of mail to go through. I just haven't gotten around to it."

"Have you been to Australia in the last three months?" Bob asked

"I returned just two and a half weeks ago."

Bob handed her a flyer. "Did you encounter the man in this picture?"

Maggie waited a few moments and then said, "Yes."

What name did he use?""

"Jameson Kanger."

"Was he on your tour?"

The suspect didn't answer for almost a minute. "Yes, he was a co-leader on the northern section of our birding tour."

"Did you see anyone named Hammond or Porky Frank?"

Maggie sighed before answering. "Yes, he was a member of our tour group."

"Have you seen either of these men since your return home?"

Maggie hesitated and gazed at the ceiling, and Bob sensed he was onto something. "I repeat, have you seen either of these men since you got home?"

Tears came down Maggie's cheeks. "Yes." At this moment, John Withers opened the door and asked Bob to step out. Outside, he told him the fingerprints did not provide a match.

Back with Maggie, Bob asked, "Have you ever heard Kanger or Frank mention a bird named Eskimo curlew?"

Maggie stammered. "Y-Y-Yes. Porky mentioned that bird again when he stayed with me. He left a suitcase with me. It had a brochure that mentioned it.""

Bob asked Steve to step outside with him, and they left the room. "Go ask Chief Henderson to get a search warrant for Smith's house while I keep her here."

"Chief," Steve said when he followed Bob's instructions. "We have a good lead, and we need a search warrant in a hurry. Margaret Smith admits to knowing both our victims and having heard them talk about Eskimo curlews. We'd like to search her home for evidence. Could you use your pull to get us a search warrant fast?"

"I'll get right to it. I know just the judge.to ask. Hold her here as long as you're able."

Back at the interrogation, Steve asked Bob to step out of the room with him. Outside he asked if Margaret had admitted knowing anything else.

"She apparently knew Frank well. She usually calls him Porky, and she claims she didn't know he's dead. Some of what she said and the way she said it caused me to think she and Frank were close."

"Henderson's trying to get a search warrant now, and he says to keep her here as long as possible."

Bob told Steve he had plenty of questions. "Stay with the Chief and execute the warrant as soon as you can while I question her."

The questioning of Maggie continued, and for a while she managed to maintain a modicum of composure, but when Bob described the state of Frank's body when he and Steve had found it covered in blood from deep knife wounds, Maggie couldn't help crying. She tried to stop and pulled a handkerchief from the pocket of her slacks and buried her head in it, muttering, "Poor Porky," over and over.

When she stopped crying, Bob asked her if she had any idea who would want to kill Frank. She remained silent for a long time. The detective waited without saying anything. Finally, he told Maggie the police were in the process of searching her house, and it would be to her advantage to cooperate with any information she had. "I repeat, do you know anybody who might have murdered Hammond Frank? Porky?"

"I'm afraid he might kill me too."

"We'll provide you protection if you cooperate. If you know who this person is, you're already in danger."

Maggie did not say anything else for a long time—waiting for him to repeat the question, pleased to be fulfilling her goal of protecting Patsy. Bob sat silent, content with keeping her at the station.

After around a quarter of an hour, Maggie spoke. "There's only one person I know of who would do something you've described. His name is Mackensie Craft. His nickname is Mack the Knife."

Detective Bruce was elated. They had Mackensie Craft on their list of people who had not returned the flyer. They would interview him the next da

"Do you know Patricia Shaper?"

"Yes."

"We're holding her for the murder of Porky."

"She didn't do it."

"We know she was at the scene. If she didn't kill Frank, she knows who did. You should tell her to cooperate. "

The questioning continued for another hour. Then Withers put his head in the room and told Bob the search had been completed,

"For the time being, we're going to let you go home," Bob said. "But you must stay in town," Bob said. "Your home has been searched. "We found evidence; don't try to leave town.

We'll put a guard on duty to protect you. If you talk to Ms. Shaper, you should encourage her to cooperate with us, if she's innocent."

"I know she didn't do it. She told me Porky was alive when she ran to her car."

"Tell her she won't be safe. If the killer knows she's alive, he'll try to kill her. She's the only witness against him."

Chapter Sixteen

When the time arrived for the interview with Mackensie Craft, the suspect did not appear. After waiting for twenty minutes, Bruce asked Chief Henderson for a warrant to allow him to take John Withers and a couple of other uniformed officers and proceed to search Craft's listed address and, if possible, apprehend him, since he appeared to be at least one of the killers. "I'm afraid he'll be gone, but perhaps we'll get lucky," Bob said.

When they reached the address listed for Craft, odor of marijuana permeated the hallway at his apartment. Nobody answered Bob's knocks on his apartment door. Bob's second round of knocks on the door also went unanswered. He knocked a third time with no success.

He and Steve drew their weapons. "Break the door in," Bob said as he motioned to two uniformed policemen. Inside, they found nobody. Steve looked through all of the rooms. "Nobody's here except us."

John Withers began searching for fingerprints. "Apparently he didn't want to see us. He didn't leave very long ago. There are almost fresh dishes in the sink. I'll see what fingerprints I can find."

"Search for anything to give us a clue where to find him," Bob said.

"He didn't want to talk to us, but he left us plenty of fingerprints," Withers said as began to collect fingerprints and compare them with the unidentified set of their mystery prints. It didn't take him long to conclude that he had a match. "We hit the jackpot on prints," he told Bob.

Bob told the uniformed officers they needed to look for Craft's knife. "He probably has the murder weapon with him, but he might have more than one."

"I'll call in to put out a BOLA for him," Steve said. "Armed and dangerous."

Bob nodded. "He has a record of violence. He's murder and mayhem walking the streets until he's apprehended."

Bruce considered their situation. "We've made a lot of progress, but we still don't know the motives of our murderers. We have to catch Craft, and we still have to discover what our killers' motivations were if we're to build a solid case. That means we have to figure out what the Eskimo curlew has to do with the killings."

Steve nodded. "Maybe Frank's suitcase we found at Margaret Smith's will help us out there."

"I hope so, but we also need to get Patricia Shaper to talk. Margaret Smith claims her friend is innocent. I don't picture her as a killer, but she has a role in whatever happened. We need to check the airports and ships leaving the area. I'd say Mack the Knife is buying a ticket right now under some alias. He's bound to be guilty of murder, but we have to catch him."

Despite his intelligence and his sophisticated tastes, Detective Robert Bruce had a faulty understanding of his quarry, whom he thought was seeking to escape by leaving the island. Bob was partially right about the ticket. Mackensie Craft had bought a plane ticket to Brazil, under his own name, but evidently not to use, rather to confuse pursuers,

ಉ   ಉ   ಉ

Mackensie Craft (or rather now Simon Wulf) had begun preparing an alternate identity as soon as he made his escape from the murder scene in the boat Kanger and Frank had been using— actually two false identities to elude the lawmen who would be searching for him. He had no desire to spend his life running from the law. Instead, he was busy carrying out a plan of disappearance on the island. He had had time to think about how to live on Galveston incognito. He would hide among the constant flood of tourists. The thought of spending his time outwitting the minions of the law appealed to him. It would be a way to enjoy what lately had been his very lonely life. Craft/Wulf had been working on changing his appearance and identity even as he butchered the body of Porky Frank with his hunting knife, a deed done for several reasons. The shotgun didn't finish the job. Even though he enjoyed the cutting, Craft wanted the police and anybody else involved to think a madman was responsible. He had sold his Honda Accord as Mackensie Craft and then had bought with cash a used Ford Fusion from a car dealer as Simon Wolf. That and what he had taken from Hammond left him with some extra cash to help finance his transition to a new life.

Simon was sure the police would be after him. He cursed himself for failing to control his rage and leaving the shotgun at the site of the murder. Such carelessness was unlike him. He suspected they would catch him right away if he obeyed the summons to an interview. He should have thrown the shotgun in the bay after he clubbed Kanger.

Simon had had a yen for violence, but he wasn't about to plead insanity. The shotgun was an accident created by that nutty lesbian, Patricia Shaper, but he'd been happy to finish the job with his knife. "What a great carving job," he told himself. He laughed. Nobody could accuse him of lacking a sense of humor. It was something he had inherited from his mother, who used to laugh as she beat and burnt him for no good reason.

When he cried and asked why he was beaten, his mother had always said, "Because it's fun for me." She was half-drunk and laughing like crazy. If Simon's father intervened, she beat him too. 'Maybe that's why I want to rape a woman whenever I recall it,'" he thought, although he didn't have pleasant memories of his father either. He was a weak drunk without courage. Thoughts of him inspired his son to resolve never to be that weak—or drunk.

Simon wanted to challenge the police, not run from them. He had been eluding them for years as he committed his rapes. He procured all the paperwork for his created identities—two new ID's, new credit cards, two new social security numbers, and a new address. One identity would allow him to live a normal life as Simon Wulf; the other would allow him to slip into the world of the homeless folk who make the island their home. As Lilac Hopper, who existed only as a post office box, he wore a blond wig and falsies when he rented her post office box and picked up her mail. That accomplished, a few days later, as Lilac Hopper, he dropped off a forwarding address card for mail from his Mackensie Craft box to be forwarded to Lilac Hopper. He knew he was taking a chance, but he thought Lilac could disappear soon enough for him to elude the police.

Simon Wulf had already rented a trailer for $250.00 a month to establish his second new address with a postal address, and he had moved all of the things he wanted to keep with him to his trailer and a storage shed he had rented under his assumed name of Simon Wulf. He paid his first trailer and storage bills with the stash of cash he'd taken off of Porky and Jameson and what he had made selling his Accord. By the time that ran out, he'd have figured out something else to do for money, and soon he would be using his new credit cards and funds sent to Lilac Hopper and forwarded to Simon Wulf.

During his changeover, he would confine himself to cash transactions as much as possible. He might even get a job eventually, but he had to prepare a resumé before applying for work somewhere. He could live off of his investments for a long time. He'd try to pose as a model citizen, but that meant he'd have to control his violence. Maybe he could get by with a rape or two now and then when the urge built up, if he were careful.

Looking at himself in the mirror, he appraised his grey beard and hair. All he had had to do to create that elderly image was to stop using hair dye and let his beard grow. Prematurely gray, Simon Wulf looked twenty years older than Mackensie Craft, but the fellow in the mirror was too good-looking. Simon Wulf would acquire a tan, let his undyed hair grow, and become a beach bum. For that purpose, he had bought a large supply of sunscreen and tanning oil. He had to give up birding except at the beach. If all went well, Simon Wulf would gradually expand his birding range once the police had stopped looking for him actively.

To begin, he'd have to limit himself to birds of the beach, but that would be his major sacrifice. Getting even with Frank and Kanger was worth the sacrifice. That scum wouldn't trick anybody else into sullying a life list. Damn them for ruining the cleanliness of his list. The disgrace of his having bragged about listing an Eskimo curlew still rankled, even after he'd settled the score.

At least he'd given that poor little curlew an end to its unhappy captivity with the second shell in the shotgun before he used it to club Kanger and use the boat for a getaway. As he decided later when his rage abated, he had been careless.

—

Bob Roberts was happy they had made so much progress with the case, but they couldn't wrap up the case unless Patricia Shaper would tell her part in the murders and they could catch Mackensie Craft. Margaret Smith had told them when she broke down in tears that Ms. Shaper did not kill Kanger or Frank. So Bob proposed they offer Shaper a deal, through her lawyer, if she would tell them exactly what happened at the time of the killings. They believed Mackensie Craft had killed Hammond Frank and Jameson Kanger, but they needed to know how Patricia's prints got on one of the murder weapons. If she could provide them with a satisfactory explanation, they'd drop the charges against her in turn for her becoming their star witness against Craft.

—

A small, slender man with curly black hair. Patsy's lawyer, Josef Jabitts, thought the police had offered his client a good deal. "I.. ah think...ah. the police have made you ...er ," he stuttered. "an offer ... ah you should take." Patsy was not impressed by her defender's presentation, but the offer of immunity if she would describe what happened at the time of the murder appealed to her. "Are you willing to be a witness for the p-p-prosecution?"

"What do you recommend?"

Emboldened by her confidence in him, Jabitts answered without a stutter. "If you tell them what you told me, you can have the case against you dismissed, or at the least, spend a year or two on probation. It's certainly worth a try. As it is, they can prosecute you for double homicide. If they find out you are pregnant from Kanger's rape, they'll have motive as well as your prints on the shotgun," Jabitts said. "The police are eager to get your testimony against Craft, but an ambitious prosecutor might see your case as a way to build a reputation."

"But I'd be at the mercy of the police," she said.

"The police believe Craft's guilty, but a competent prosecutor could convict you if Craft isn't available. These guys are offering you a way out. They say your friend, Margaret Smith, who was close to Frank, says you're innocent. I recommend you grab the lifeline they're throwing you."

Patsy thought it over and discussed it with Maggie, when her friend visited her.

"Honey, they're offering you a way out. They know Mack carved up Porky. If you tell them what you told me, they'll let you go," Maggie said.

So Patsy agreed to tell her story, even though it would reveal her motive for wanting to kill Jameson. Bob conducted the interview with Steve and Jabitts observing. "Ms. Shaper, as you can see, I'm recording this. Do I have your permission?"

"Yes, I'm giving this statement on the advice of my attorney."

"Then we'll proceed. Why did you happen to be at the scene of the murder of Frank and Kanger."

"I knew that Kanger was going to be there. I'd been approached about paying to see a wild Eskimo curlew, but knowing the two of them were up to something, I turned down their way-too-expensive offer. I went to meet Kanger, who had raped me in Australia. I was pregnant by him and went there to confront him. He laughed at me when I told him. He offered to fuck me until I miscarried. I became so angry I yelled at him and hit him a couple of times with my fists.

"Porky heard us and came around the trees to see what was wrong. 'You two shut up. You're scaring the bird,' he said. He and Kanger went around to the other side of the copse. I saw a shotgun in the boat they'd used to set up the scam. I grabbed it and followed them back.

"When I got around to the other side, Mackensie Craft was accusing Porky of trickery and was threatening him with a knife. Porky and Jameson turned when they saw me with the shotgun. Craft was cursing. 'You son of a bitch,' he said to Porky. 'You promised me a view of a wild, unrestrained Eskimo curlew, but this bird is tethered. It's probably not an Eskimo curlew either, you conniving bastard. I've already paid you over two thousand dollars. I want my money back.' "I pointed the shotgun at Kanger, but he ducked behind Mack, who took hold of the gun and pointed its barrel at Porky, who reached out for the gun."

Patricia paused; "Could I have some water? Or coffee? "

Steve said, "Sure, I'll bring you some water."

After Patricia had drunk half the cup, she continued. "Mack ended up with the gun as it went off, and Porky fell to the ground. By this time, Jameson was trying to wrest the shotgun from Mack, who clubbed him on the head with the butt of the gun, but Jameson managed to stagger away from Mack, who used the other shot in the gun to kill the little curlew.

"I guess the two of them kept fighting and dropped the gun on the way back to the boat. I ran to my car as fast as I could. I guess Kanger collapsed in the marsh before he could get the boat into the water. As far as I know Jameson and Porky were alive when I got away, running as fast as I could."

"Craft must have used the boat for his getaway," Bob said. Bob and Steve agreed that her story seemed plausible. "Ms. Shaper," Bob said, "we both think your narrative has a ring of truth. It fits the evidence we have. We'll arrange to drop charges against you, but you'll have to remain here in Galveston until we complete the paperwork and bring Craft to trial. You must testify against him. You must keep yourself available for further questioning and testimony against Craft at his trial.

"If you should hear from Mr. Craft, please be sure to call us. He will try to kill you. We'll assign an officer to guard you. Your statement should protect you somewhat, but, he might not think about that. We'll let it be known to the press you've made a statement, and we are keeping you under protection."

"Thank you, Detective. I'm going to stay with my friend, Maggie, for a while, and I plan to keep a gun handy for protection."

Chapter Seventeen

Bob Bruce and Steve Jackson were confident they had solved the case, but they were disappointed that the murderer had so far eluded arrest. Apparently he had wanted them to believe he'd fled to Brazil. He had bought the ticket, but nobody used it. The stewardess remembered the flight was full except for that seat, and a very happy stand-by was put in it.

"He may still be somewhere in the United States," Bob said.

Steve unwrapped a stick of chewing gum and offered a stick to Bob. "Do you suppose he could still be in Galveston?"

Popping gum in his mouth, Bob stood. "A person who did what he did could do almost anything. He probably enjoyed carving Frank's body. I believe he might try to stay here. What his history suggests to me is that, if he's here, we're going to deal with some more violent crimes done by him."

"I don't doubt that, but how would you know whether Craft is the perp?"

Bob explained his hunch. "I believe he may be the serial rapist, who always uses a knife. It's just a gut feeling. Frank's killer didn't show the cautious established pattern the rapist uses, but we don't know of any copycat rapes so far since the murders. We have his fingerprints from the murders. If he is the rapist, he slipped up murdering Frank and Kanger and leaving the shotgun. He might slip again. If he's here, I'll bet he'll try to rape and kill Patricia Shaper. She can place him at the scene of the murders at the time they happened. Nobody else can. We need to keep an eye on her. And we should suspect him of any horrific violence with a knife on the island."

⁋ ⁋ ⁋

Unknown to Bob and Steve, Mackensie Craft/Simon Wulf had begun stalking Patsy and had become aware of her special relationship with Margaret Smith. Acting on this knowledge, Simon began to follow both of them, learning their habits and planning how best to strike up an acquaintance with Smith. He had seen her at Birds & Floats. She was an enthusiastic beginning bird watcher. She wasn't bad looking, Simon thought. He had always had a yen for good-looking blondes. He wouldn't mind bedding her while he developed his plans for Shaper. His opportunity to meet Margaret arrived when she came down to the beach near Resthaven Trailer Park, an eighth of a mile from Woody's beer joint near Pocket Park One—just a short walk from Simon's Trailer 10.

It was a was a sunny morning. He spotted his quarry from the back of his trailer. He had named it "Serendipity," Simon looked down to the beach from his trailer. Smith was with Shaper. They both were using binoculars, evidently trying to identify the gulls, terns, and shorebirds—a perfect opportunity to test his disguise on Patsy, test Smith, and do a little birding at the same time.

Dressed in shorts, tee-shirt, sandals, and binoculars, Simon strode out to the beach, lifting his optics now and then to identify a bird. He moved toward the two women. He edged closer and closer. As the three of them were watching a group of terns, Simon pretended to lose a flip-flop and stumble, catching himself in front of Margaret. "Oh, clumsy of me, I'm sorry." he said as he straightened up next to her. "It's a nice batch of terns. Are you ladies watching the birds too?"

"Yes, there're so many of them this morning," Margaret said.

"Are you pretty good at identifying terns and gulls?" Patricia Shaper asked.

Simon beamed at them. "Not to brag, but I'm pretty good with beach birds," he said. He could see no evidence that Shaper recognized him. His disguise seemed to be effective, but it needed further testing.

"Would you help us identify them?" Margaret asked.

Simon bowed and saluted them with a flourish of his arm. "My pleasure, Dear Lady." He pointed out the large terns first. "Those large white birds with the heavy yellow bills are royal terns." He was enjoying his charade. Apparently, his disguise was good enough to fool Shaper and Smith. He strove to conceal his glee.

Focusing on the yellow bills, Shaper said, "They're pretty."

"Now look through those until you find one a little larger with a heavier blood-red bill. It has a crew cut instead a of a black tuft at the back of its crest. That's a Caspian tern, the world's largest."

"I see it. That huge bill is blood red," said Margaret.

Simon continued through the flock of birds, identifying more than twenty species of terns, gulls, herons, and small shorebirds, enjoying his task, displaying his knowledge as he gained the confidence of the women, who in a short time became Maggie and Patsy to him as he became Simon to them.

By late morning, they had begun to notice the heat. "Ladies," Simon said, "I'm thirsty. Let me treat you to drinks at Woody's."

"That's a great idea," Maggie said. "Unless Patsy objects, I'll accept for us both." Simon took her arm in his.

Patsy hesitated for a minute or so, "I don't know that I should," she said, but then waved her hand. "I guess it's okay," she said, taking Maggie's other arm.

Linked arm in arm, they climbed the wide steps to the elevated porch at Woody's and sat at a table in the shade of the roof. "I'm going to have a beer. What'll you ladies have? It's on me," Simon said. Maggie said she'd have beer too, but Patsy ordered a coke.

As they drank, Maggie questioned Simon. "Do you spend much time at the beach. You have a good tan. I hope you use sun screen."

Simon laughed. "I use so much sun tan oil and sunscreen I'm thinking of investing in them. I rent a trailer in The Resthaven Trailer Park. Some people there call me a beach bum."

Maggie examined him with an intense gaze for several seconds. "Your tan becomes you. You remind me of those handsome men in the liquor advertisements. What do you think, Patsy?"

Simon wondered if the gray moustache and well-trimmed gray beard he now sported would survive this challenge.

"Leave me out of this," the Olympian said.

"Oh, come on, be a sport," Maggie teased.

Patsy screwed up her face and bent her head sideways, pretending to judge Simon's demeanor. "Maybe, his hair is a little long, but if you give him a haircut and put him in a gray suit with a nice tie, he could hold a glass of whiskey and pass for a man of distinction."

Simon laughed. "You lovely ladies are too kind. Do you come to the beach often?"

"We'll come more often if you promise to show us the birds," Maggie said.

"I'll be glad to do that. Just let me know when. I'm in Trailer 10."

After they had finished their drinks, Simon took Maggie's address and phone number and gave his. He said his goodbyes to them after agreeing to watch birds with them again the next week.

A cheerful Simon walked back down the beach to his trailer, pleased that he had made friends with Margaret Smith and that his disguise had fooled her and Patsy. He must study her to prepare for his attack. He would wait until his urge to rape became unbearable. "I want to lull the police into thinking their suspect has gone elsewhere," he said to himself. "In the meantime, I'll see what I can arrange with Maggie. I'm delighted Shaper hasn't recognized me. I can take my time with her—since she doesn't suspect who I really am." Hiding from the police might turn out to be great fun. He knew he was taking a dangerous chance, but he was enjoying outwitting his pursuers too much to quit and leave town.

⁋ ⁋ ⁋

"Don't you think you're rushing things. We don't know anything about this Wulf guy. The police warned us, especially me, to be on the guard about strangers," Patsy said as she and Maggie settled down to sandwiches at Maggie's.

"I guess you're right, but he seems likable. He certainly is handsome. I don't propose to stop enjoying life just because the Galveston police can't apprehend the killer of Porky and Kanger."

"Well, you and I have become good friends. You've given me good advice, but I believe the police when they say that Craft, if he's still around, will try to kill me. It makes sense to be wary of men who suddenly materialize. He's appeared from nowhere."

"I know you need to be careful, but I'm going to find out more about Simon Wulf. He seems to be okay. He's good company."

"Then why don't we know anything about him? A birder of his expertise should be well known in Galveston birding circles. if he's from out of town, he may be okay, but I'm staying away from him."

૎ ૎ ૎

Simon didn't waste time putting his plan into effect. He thought four days a long enough wait. Then he called Maggie and asked if she would take a walk on the beach with him that evening, just the two of them, then have a burger and beer at Michaelburger's.

"That sounds like fun," Maggie said.

"I'll pick you up around six then. I'll be in a green Ford Fusion. Bring your binoculars."

"I'll be ready."

Maggie told Patsy about the date with Simon. "We're going down to the beach."

"I think you should be careful," Patsy said. "We don't know much about Simon Wulf. He seems to have sprung out of nowhere. How come we don't know anything about a birder as good as he is? Something about him seems familiar to me. Remember the warning the police gave us?"

"You're probably right, but I'll be careful," Maggie said. She thought Patsy might be a little jealous, even though the police had warned them. Simon didn't seem to be a murderer. After all, not many birders are. She'd find out where he was from. He was bound to be from out of town.

As Simon and Maggie walked down the beach, he pointed out the birds for her. "It certainly is fun to walk with you identifying the birds," Maggie said.

Putting his arm around her, he pulled her closer, "It gives me pleasure to please you," Simon said, as he pointed out a flock of Foster's terns hunting their supper out over the Gulf. He pulled out the beach towel he had brought in his backpack and spread it on the sand. "Let's sit awhile in the fading sunlight, Smell that salt tang of the sea breeze."

As they sat and watched the birds and the declining sun, She snuggled against him. "The sea breeze feels good," she said. "You seem to be from out of town. Where do you hail from?"

"I moved here from Norfolk, Virginia, after I got out of the navy."

"Were you an officer?"

"No, just a warramt officer."

"Aren't they officers?"

"I was a Purser. I handled the money." He smiled. "I learned enough about finances that I've made a lot of money in the stock market. We've just met, but I feel like we're old friends," Simon said. as he planted a kiss on Maggie's lips.

"I feel that way, too, Simon.," she said as she pressed his hand in hers, "but we've just met, and I still don't know much about you." She couldn't help remembering Patsy's forebodings.

"Look, look up to the left," Simon pointed with his free hand, "there's a young frigatebird soaring our way. See its white belly. What a great sight."

"He's not even flapping a wing. It's amazing. I've never seen one before."

"They're great soaring machines. What wouldn't I give to be able to fly like that."

They watched the man-o-war bird sail down the beach and out of sight, then watched gulls and terns fishing as the sun gave way to dusk, and a flock of pelicans sailed overhead. Simon stretched out on the beach towel and pulled her down facing him and kissed her again as he pressed her against him.

Maggie pulled back. "Simon, I can tell you're excited. I'm glad I have that effect on you, but I think we'd better walk over and get that burger you promised me. I'm hungry."

Simon stood and pulled Maggie up. "Help me shake the towel and put it in my back pack. I'm getting hungry too."

After a short walk, they crossed the highway and ordered Michaelburgers and beers. SImon raised his beer. "Here's to our growing friendship."

"I'll drink to that," Maggie said, lifting her beer to clink mugs. "I 've had fun whenever we've been together." They made short work of their meal and headed back down the beach, now covered with moonlight, walking hand in hand and making frequent stops. A short drive to Maggie's ended with another kiss.

Patsy greeted Maggie at the door. "I'm glad to see you're okay. I keep thinking there's something about Simon Wulf that seems very familiar to me. I think I'm going to sleep with my shotgun handy from now on."

"Simon says he was a warrant officer in the navy. He moved here from Norfolk, Virginia, when he retired. He seems like such a nice man, but you're right to be cautious. The police warned us to be suspicious. Come have a cola; I'll have one too. I'll put some rum in them." Maggie said. "I think we could both use a little something in our drinks. Simon's the first man I've had any use for since Porky. I hope he's okay."

"I know. I don't like to rain on your straight love life. I can tell you like him, but I'll do what I can to take your mind off him; I might be a little jealous, but the police warned me to be careful." Patsy said as she gave Maggie a kiss. "I don't want to die."

"I don't think Simon is dangerous. Let's have some margaritas and go to bed. Simon and I had burgers. I'll fix you a ham and tomato sandwich. I'll try to make you forget about Simon," Maggie said.

Chapter Eighteen

In the midst of fitful sleep, Simon muttered as one of his dreadful nightmares brought forth memories of his childhood, when he was four or five. A grown-up woman (his mother) is pressing her burning cigarette against the boy's naked flesh, and he is crying.

"Bring me muh bottle or I'll press and burn where it will hurt more," she says, turning up her glass to show it's empty. Drying his tears with his arm, the little boy brings her a half-full bottle of whiskey. "Thas a good boy," the woman says and fills her glass and sips. Pushing aside her gown, she pulls the boy to her, "Now ya can kiss Mommy's breast. "Suck it nice." She laughed. "mite get some milk."

The ugly dream shifts to an older boy, eleven or twelve, being burned by a cigarette applied to his scrotum and pubic hair by a woman lying on a couch..

"Ohh,.. damn, that hurts, you drunk bitch," he cries and writhes in pain. The woman slaps him. "Don'cha sass yoh ma. Bring me muh pills and some water." The boy brings her a container with pills and a glass of water. The woman puts some whiskey in the water, takes her pills and washes them down. "Thas a good boy. Now kiss Mommy." She puts aside her gown, "Kiss ...use ya tongue .. thass right."

The scene shifts again. The woman is switching the naked boy with a limber rod front and back as he tries to protect himself. "Thas the way to jump," she laughs, as he cries when a particularly vicious blow hits his privates.

"You bitch, I did what you asked. I brought you your whiskey and did those other things you like."

"Nod long enough. Do mouh," she said as she drops the rod and pulls him to her.

₭   ₭   ₭

Awake in his bed at Resthaven, Simon tries to forget his nightmare and congratulates himself on how well his plan about Patricia Shafer was playing out, and how much pleasure it was to implement. Maggie reminded him of the neighborhood woman who had introduced him to pleasant sex when he was fifteen. She was a widow.

"You remind me of my husband when we were teenagers," she said. In her early fifties, she could pass for much younger. He hadn't given up his paper route and had stopped by on his bicycle to collect for the month. He was wearing a t-shirt and loose running pants. After she paid him, she asked him to stay and have some pop and cookies she'd just baked. He accepted, and she brought out a dozen chocolate chip cookies and a cola.

Dressed in a loose housecoat, she bent down to place the cookies on the coffee table in front of the sofa he was sitting on. Her housecoat flopped open, revealing her nakedness underneath.

"You're pretty," he said as he tried to hide his erection as she tied her robe.

"Thank you," she said as she reached out to touch him peeping out of his shorts. "Do you have a girlfriend?"

He wondered how to answer. Blushing, he finally said, "No…No ma'am."

"I'll bet you're a virgin," she said. She sat down beside him, took his free hand and put it on her breast while she pulled down his shorts. Several hours and lessons later he no longer was a virgin and had begun his complex relationship with older women who, unlike his mother, were loving and caring instead of cruel. Maggie reminded him of that lady with the cookies. The irony did not escape him but did little to relieve his suppressed anger.

He'd have to spend a lot of time following Patricia's goings and comings, to learn her habits, but he'd be able to mix pleasure with Maggie in his preparations for revenge on Patricia, and he wanted to hold off on that as long as possible to fool the police. He should kill Patricia. He felt wretched when he thought about how to get rid of her. He didn't like hating women, but his memories of his childhood kept building up and demanding vengeance. And Patricia was a threat. So far she hadn't recognized him, but he didn't know how long that would last. She certainly wasn't as eager to be a friend of his as Maggie was.

That friendship progressed with weekly bird watching at the beach, but Patsy never joined them. Maggie made excuses, telling Simon that the police had warned her friend to stay where they could guard her. To keep both friendships, Maggie made notes on her calendar to make sure her dates with Simon did not overlap with engagements she made with Patsy, who often sat in as Maggie's bridge partner when she entertained her garden club friends. And sometimes they birded together at locations away from the beach.

After more than a month, Maggie and Simon spent a particularly pleasant morning birding at the beach, and she suggested that he have lunch with her at her home. They had a lunch of ham and cheese sandwiches and a vegetable soup in the kitchen. After they ate, Maggie excused herself. After a few minutes later she reappeared wearing only a bra and panties under a see-through nightgown.

"I'm wondering, am I to have more than sandwiches and soup for lunch?" Simon asked, preparing himself for the test.

"There may be some other things for dessert, but that depends on you. I want to know something more about you. You haven't said much about yourself."

Simon followed her into the kitchen, where Maggie mixed drinks of cola and rum. Then she led him to her sofa in her front room, bringing a tray with more cola and rum with them and set it down on the coffee table in front of the sofa.

"There's not much to tell about me," Simon said. "I saved money and made wise investments for twenty years while I served in the navy. By then I had more than enough to live on. So I retired from the navy and became a financial planner. After a few years I limited that work to two days a week and spent my time birding. That's when I moved to Galveston."

"You haven't been very active in birding circles here so far. Why not?"

"Well, I'm still very new in Galveston. I've been busy getting settled. I've been getting used to the beach birds."

Sitting on the sofa, Maggie kicked off her slippers and pulled Simon down beside her. "This has been a lovely day," she said. "I don't want it to end."

Simon put his drink on the coffee table. ""You seem to bring out the best in me. I can't explain it." He shook his head, surprised by this self-knowledge coming into his mind. "Don't talk about its ending. It's still young. You mix a delicious drink," he said. It was a great coke. A second was breaking down his wall of caution.

"Can you tell me a little more about yourself?"

"It's a long uninteresting story about how my investments made me a millionaire. I've been a lucky stock picker."

Maggie sighed. "Let's make this a long, long afternoon," she said. She thought such financial success precluded his being a murderer.

⁊ ⁊ ⁊

Back at hid Resthaven trailer, Simon continued to plan his next nighttime activity well in advance. His tension had increased as he had feared, and his nightmares were increasing in frequency. The knowledge that Patsy had witnessed his murder of Porky and Jameson added to his tension. A week later he decided he needed to push his schedule forward.

He'd move up his nighttime visit to Patricia's two-bedroom apartment north of Heard's Lane. His visits would be over before she recognized him. He would alter his leave-taking ritual. He would conclude his visit by killing her after her shower. The consciousness of the need to kill bothered him, but he continued his preparations. He used a couple of nights before the final night to see what the latest police surveillance of Shaper was like.

With his destination in mind, he consulted his checklist and began to lay out his special outfit: a black hood revealing only his eyes and mouth, black shirt and pants, black jacket, black boots and socks, and black gloves. His equipment included a black twenty-two revolver, his black-handled hunting knife, and a voice disguiser. He also included matches and cigarettes and a lighter—small items he put in a black waist pack.

In a plastic bag stuffed inside the larger bag he put condoms, a small container of liquid soap for her shower after sex, toothpaste, toothbrush, and mouthwash, and paper towels for wiping, K-y jelly away. In a backpack he put a roll of duct tape and several folded large black plastic garbage bags..

Preparing, he rehearsed in his mind the series of actions he intended to require of his victim, actions designed to intimidate and terrorize her and thus satisfy him. He had been watching his victim's ground-floor apartment for weeks and trying the windows. One in a room next to her bedroom he had found always open. He'd abort action if it happened to be locked the night he had chosen. Patricia slept in the room adjacent to the one with the open window. Such carelessness... he deplored her making his task so easy.

So he spent several more nights investigating the neighborhood around Patricia's apartment. He took notes on the comings and goings of the police assigned to protect her. Reviewing these notes, he concluded he had a sufficient time to slip in between midnight and two o'clock in the morning. He kept track of the nights she slept at home. He still hated to think of killing her, but it was necessary to protect himself. He steeled himself to necessity. After all, he was already guilty of two murders. The added penalty for one more wouldn't be that great.

Friday night a week later, before midnight, he dressed and put his equipment in his car and headed for his victim's neighborhood. He parked on a street several blocks over from his victim's house—between a couple of black trucks— and walked to his victim's apartment, avoiding people and animals. He did not see anybody watching. He was lucky. The window was open. He put through his backpack and crawled through without making any noise. Inside, he proceeded quietly to Patsy's bedroom. His eyes had adjusted to the dark, and he could see her in the bed, seemingly asleep on her left side.

Putting the duct tape in his pants pocket, he pulled his

hunting knife from its sheath and crept to the bed, pulling Patsy over on her back. He kneeled over her, straddling her nakedness at her waist, and holding the knife to her throat. "Wake up!" demanded in his altered voice as he pulled out the tape and pressed several large pieces over her mouth while she was awaking. "I won't hurt you if you do what I order you to do. If not, I can use this knife or the revolver I've brought," the altered voice commanded. Approving what he considered a proper fright on her face, he put a couple of extra pillows behind her.

"I'm going to take the tape off your mouth now. You'd better be quiet. I could kill you quickly with this knife." He pressed it against her throat. For the next hour he subjected her to terror and sexual humiliation with burning cigarettes and numerous sexual acts using all the portals of her body, all the time with the hunting knife threatening to strike and using condoms to collect his semen. After the final anal punishment, he put all the evidence in plastic zip-lock bags.

"Now it's time to clean up with a shower," he said. "First, pull off the sheets and put them in these plastic garbage bags. The pillow cases too." When Patsy was slowly carrying out that chore, she reached under the bed and grasped her loaded double-barreled Mossaberg 930 Watchdog semi-automatic shotgun hidden there. Rising up, she dropped the sheet covering the gun, pointing it at the rapist, who approached holding his knife as he advanced.

"Drop that knife."

He kept moving toward her, brandishing the knife. She shot the arm holding the knife, which clattered to the floor. He snarled his pain,

"Get out of my house, you bastard, before I use the next shot to kill you," Patsy ordered. He paused. "Now! Get out, you son of a bitch, or my next shot will kill you or leave you impotent." Without saying another word, he picked up the knife and his bags and fled.

His victim picked up some shells from her stash and followed him, to make sure he left. Once he climbed out the window where he entered and ran, she fired another shot at his fleeing figure, aiming at his buttocks, but missing, as he changed direction.

The policeman assigned to protect Patricia heard the gunshots just as he returned from break and hurried to investigate. He rang the doorbell., Shaper threw on a housecoat and answered the door. "Hello, Officer. You're a little late. I've already been raped, but I wounded the son of a bitch and chased him off. I think he was planning ro kill me."

— — —

Saturday night Patsy answered the door when Simon rang the doorbell at Maggie's. Maggie had prevailed upon her to accept an invitation to a spaghetti dinner with her even though Simon was to be there too. Not wanting to be alone, Patsy had agreed after considerable hesitation. She answered the door while Maggie finished preparing the meal. Patsy was surprised to see Simon was wearing a long-sleeved shirt.

"It's a little warm for that shirt, don't you think?"

"I had a little accident in the kitchen fixing lunch."

She noticed what might have been a little blood had soiled one sleeve on the lower right. "Did you hurt your arm?"

"Yes, just a scratch—a cooking accident."

"Did he cut himself?" Patsy said to herself. She examined his arm— trying to keep her interest hidden. "I've seen a birthmark like the one on his hand before," she said to herself. "Where?"

"Do you have an allergy?" Simon asked. "There's redness around your eyes."

"No, I've been crying," she said without offering any details.

She ushered him into the room Maggie called her dining room, where three places were already set and a big bowl of salad sat in the middle of the table beside salad dressings, other condiments, and a container of grated cheese. Patsy said, "Maggie wants you to sit down. Fix yourself a salad. We'll bring in the sauce and noodles."

Dinner began with Maggie's filling plates with spaghetti noodles and garlic bread while Patsy passed the sauce to Simon. Then Maggie poured some red wine for each of them. The supper was delicious, and everyone finished in not much more than one refill of wine.

"That was a great meal," Simon said.

"Time for a movie," Maggie said. She looked at Patsy to see how she reacted. Her friend didn't have any reaction that her hostess could detect. "Are you all right with that, Patsy?"

"I'm going to try to be. I don't want to spoil things, but I just can't be very upbeat. I'm hoping time will wipe away my memories of last night."

"That's my girl," Maggie said.

"What happened last night?" Simon tried to sound genuinely concerned and desirous of wanting the information.

"Patsy spent a night of terror," Maggie said. "She was raped last night. She was afraid he was going to kill her, but she was brave. She used her shotgun to get rid of him, and her police protection responded right away. When she told him she'd been raped and how, he told her she'd been attacked by the serial rapist who insists on the routine she described."

Simon mustered enough empathy to express his regrets. "I'm glad you're okay, Patsy." His lie seemed sincere.

Maggie said, "The police were very interested. They're wondering if there's any connection to the Frank murder. This was the first rape reported since then that fits the pattern of this serial rapist."

Simon didn't say anything for almost a minute, Finally, he offered his apologies for having intruded at such a time. "It was a wonderful meal, Maggie, I won't bother you and Patsy anymore tonight."

"It was no bother; Patsy didn't want to be alone."

"I wouldn't have come if I'd known. Call me when you want to go birding again." He showed himself out before Maggie could object.

Breaking the sudden silence, Patsy said, "Maybe he didn't want to sit through a movie."

"Why do you say that?"

"I think he had a wound on his arm below his elbow. His long-sleeved shirt had what might have been a little blood there. He said it was from a cooking accident. That's where I shot the rapist last night. I thought there was something familiar about Simon. The rapist had a birthmark on his hand like one Craft had, Simon has one just like it. I checked his hand tonight after I saw that blood."

"Are you sure?"

"Sure enough that I don't want to be around Simon ever again. He's all yours. I want to stay friends with you. I won't tell the police as long as he leaves me alone, but I'm not giving him another opportunity to kill me. If I'm right, I'm a witness to his murders. I'm getting a permit for a handgun to carry with me all the time."

"I'm so sorry. I don't want to lose your friendship."

"Then make sure you keep Simon and me apart."

"Let me console you tonight. You stay here with me." Maggie hugged Patsy and kissed her.

"All right. That sounds wonderful. I don't want to spend tonight alone."

℃ ℃ ℃

Simon was glad to escape Maggie's. He had enough feelings for Maggie so that he hoped he'd be able to persuade her he didn't like movies. He never knew when the urge for revenge would come upon him. He had been so busy working on shoring up his new identity. He hoped he had drained the revenge beast and kept the monster at bay. Still, he knew he couldn't fight it off forever. He ought to kill Patricia, yet last night's close call was evidence that he had to stay away from her, even though his beast might wake from its slumber. If it did, he'd find another victim. He hoped his disguise was sufficient to fool Patsy.

Several weeks later, after many more beach walks, Simon had a phone call from Maggie. "I'm fixing a spaghetti supper Saturday night a week from now for two. Can I count on you?"

"Yes, on one condition."

"What's that?"

"That I'm your only guest, and you fix lunch for me today."

Maggie laughed. "Will sandwiches and drinks do?"

"Sounds just right."

"Okay, come over at ten. You can take me birding at the beach and then we can come back here for lunch."

Simon was relieved. He thought that lunch and trimmings with

Maggie today would put him in good enough shape to keep the beast at a distance, He kept thinking he should kill Patsy. But he worried. Maybe not, that might be too dangerous now. He knew from what Maggie said that the police were watching her and Patricia in an effort to catch the killer of Frank. He had become all too aware of what a dangerous game he was playing.

Patsy was too good with a gun to take another chance. Besides, the police would check all of her windows now.

After an hour and a half of birding at the beach, Simon brought

Maggie home, they had lunch, and then they spent a pleasant afternoon

together before Maggie sent him home. He suspected Patsy was coming over for supper with Maggie, but he asked no questions.

Chapter Nineteen

s Maggie had said, the rapist's victim, Patricia Shaper, had reported the rape to the police, and her bedroom had undergone an examination, which discovered a few small pieces of the rapist's gear left in her bedroom. It became part of the evidence but did not reveal fingerprints. Two days after Patricia Shaper's report of being raped, Bob and Steve were going through their notes over numerous cups of coffee. They were considering the likelihood of Bob's hunch that the Frank murder and the serial rapes were both the work of Mackensie Craft.

Bob was now convinced the two cases were linked. "It's too much of a coincidence that Patricia Shaper, witness to the murder of Hammond Frank and Jameson Kanger, would be chosen as the first rape victim of the serial rapist after Frank's murder. She was lucky he didn't kill her. Perhaps she can give us more information. I'd say she's lucky she's a crack shot with her shotgun."

Steve nodded. "I agree. The murder may help us solve the rape case. The rapist has been too careful to leave any fingerprints or DNA. Maybe he's becoming careless. Or met his match. That Shaper woman's no coward. We must keep her under better surveillance at night in case he tries again."

Bob scratched his head. "He was interrupted by Shaper. We'll pursue the leads we have. Shaper's involved in the murder and in the rapes. If we watch her carefully, the people around her may lead us to a suspect—especially Margaret Smith. We must make sure they keep all their windows and doors locked. Unknown to them, the murderer-rapist may be within their circle of acquaintances. It's far-fetched, I admit, but I can't think of any better theory. Maybe he's slick enough to have fooled Shaper and Smith too."

"I agree. It's a way-out theory, but I can't think of anything as good," Steve said. "I agree we should look into the people Margaret Smith knows since she's a close friend of Patricia Shaper. Let's set up cameras to photograph people coming and going at Margaret Smith's house."

૏ ૏ ૏

Her party for two having been successful, Maggie decided to have an outing with Simon by herself. She couldn't believe Patsy was right about him. So the middle of the next week she called Simon and asked him if he would consider doing a weekend birding trip with her, maybe to Choke Canyon State Park. She'd drive and pay for a motel room, and they could go Dutch on the food and drink.

"I think that's a swell idea., but I'll pay for the food. What weekend do you have in mind?"

"I'd like to go this weekend, if it's agreeable to you."

"It's all right with me."

Maggie offered to include Patsy. The timing and the company did not please her. friend. "I told you I don't want to see Simon again. I'm certain he's the man who killed Porky and Jameson and raped me," Patsy said. "He had me fooled, but I told you I saw the birthmark on his hand that night at your dinner. It was just like the birthmark I saw on my rapist's hand and like the one on Mackensie Craft's hand—all in the very same place. I've had time to think about it."

"You must be mistaken. I can't imagine Simon's hurting anybody, especially me."

"He's different around you, but I 'm the only witness to his murders. I can't afford to take chances."

That same morning, Margaret Smith had a visit from Detective Robert Bruce. Bob called her first, asking if he could stop by her house and talk. She agreed, and so Bob rang her doorbell at ten o'clock that Wednesday. Maggie served him coffee and oatmeal-raisin cookies in her kitchen. "What did you want to see me about?"

"We've decided that we'd better keep a check on you since your friend Ms. Shaper was a victim of our rapist. You might be next. So we'd appreciate your keeping us informed of your movements. Nothing to worry about, just a precaution for your safety," he said.

"I appreciate your concern. That really was dreadful, what happened to Patsy. That man frightened her, and she's not scared easily. She was afraid he'd kill her, but she got the upper hand with her shotgun before he could."

"She was right to be afraid. We think he has killed. If our suspicions are correct, he killed Hammond Frank and Jameson Kanger."

"I've planned a birding trip this coming weekend with a friend, who's just moved here from Virginia after leaving the navy. We're going to Choke Canyon State Park. I'll be back by Monday."

"Be careful," Bob said as he took his leave.

& & &

Friday morning, Maggie and Simon were on the road by nine. The two had made sure their binoculars were handy in case they'd see something along the road to stop for. Maggie had packed chicken salad sandwiches and lemonade for their lunch so that they would not waste traveling time. Simon told her to keep a look out for scissor-tailed flycatchers and white-tailed hawks and other birds perched on wires at roadside. When they stopped for gas, Maggie pulled out their sandwiches and lemonade. Though they stopped a few times for looks at white-tailed hawks and kingbirds and other flycatchers perched on the wires, they got to their motel at Due West by four o clock and checked in. Maggie often looked over at her companion. He looked so handsome and kind. She couldn't believe him to be a rapist. He was more likely to have women offering themselves to him.

After finding their room and freshening up, they drove out to the park and spent several hours watching the birds in its south section, There were still a few waterfowl that hadn't gone north, and Maggie and Simon had good looks at a roadrunner and a flock of turkeys as well as green jays and kiskadee flycatchers. Simon heard a vireo he couldn't place immediately, so they spent twenty minutes finding what turned out to be a Bell's vireo. "That's a new bird for me and you too, I think," he said.

"A lot of these birds have been new for me," Maggie said. "It's so good to have you along, Simon."

"I'm having a great time too," Simon said,

"I'm getting hungry. Let's go to supper at that Tex-Mex restaurant we saw in Due West." Maggie was having a hard time believing what Patsy had told her. Although she was alarmed when she saw the birthmark Patsy had described, she still could not believe Simon was guilty of murder and rape. She had enough caution to keep quiet about what Patsy and Detective Baker had said, but she thought they must have somebody else other than Simon in mind. After all, he'd just moved to Galveston from Virginia.

After supper, Maggie requested a wake-up call from the desk at six, and then, after lovemaking, they dropped asleep entwined.

∞ ∞ ∞

Since Patricia Shaper's rape, Bob and Steve had spent their time following up on Bob's talk with Maggie and discussing where they stood with the murder and rape cases. So far they hadn't come up with much. except that a male friend of Maggie and Patsy's seemed to have materialized as a tenant at the Resthaven Trailer Park just a month or so earlier (at about the same time as Mackensie Craft had disappeared). At least that's what people around the beach near Woody's told them.

"He's been bird watching with them. He seems to be a good friend of Margaret Smith. I have difficulty thinking him the person the police are looking for," one informant told Bob. "He told us he just moved here from Virginia after he retired from the navy."

Bob called Georgina on the off chance somebody at Birds & Floats could remember Maggie's male friends.

"Hey, Sweetheart, do you know of any male bird-watching friends of Margaret Smith on the membership list of "Birds & Floats?"

"I don't remember any since her husband died. She was devoted to him. Give me a few days, and I'll ask around. I'll start with people in the office. Maggie is especially good at making friends."

Fifteen minutes passed before she returned his call.. "Honey, as far as I or the others here can remember, Maggie didn't have many friends among our male members. Why did you ask? Does it have something to do with our murders?"

"Yes, I'll tell you this evening. Are we going out for dinner?"

"No, I'm fixing salmon with rum sauce and margaritas."

Bob figured that she was planning a romantic evening. "I'm looking forward to it. Don't go too heavy on the rum."

⁢ ⁢ ⁢

Maggie answered the wake-up call at six a.m. and looked over at her bedfellow. She shoved him and woke him as she attempted to get out of bed. Awake and breakfasted, they drove to the other side of the park and birded, finding orioles, Harris's hawks, nesting verdins on territory, ash-throated flycatchers and many waders. They heard a beautiful song that began with notes sounding like a bouncing ball. Simon told Maggie it was an Olive Sparrow. They spent ten minutes getting a decent look at it, and in the process they discovered a male bronzed cowbird with his ruff puffed up. "Bad news for the sparrow and the orioles," Simon said. "Cowbirds are brood parasites."

"So they lay their eggs in other bird's nests?"

"That's right. Down here they parasitize the orioles. Up at Galveston they adopt great-tailed grackles. Nobody minds the grackles, there are so many of them."

They had a pleasant morning of birding before they felt hunger and thirst, so they pulled out the jug of water and the rest of the sandwiches Maggie had brought and drove to some benches and tables in the shade.

As they ate lunch, Maggie mentioned the visit from Detective Bruce she'd had. "The police think I might be in danger from the rapist because I'm friends with Patsy."

Simon was quiet for a minute. "I've heard that Bruce married Georgina Clayton, who runs Birds & Floats."

Maggie laughed. "The way I heard it, she married him. He just didn't put up a fight.

"Are the police still working on that murder case?" Simon asked.

"I guess so, why?

"Just curious. I haven't read about it in the papers lately."

"I heard at Birds & Floats that they solved the murder, but the murderer got away—vanished into thin air," Maggie said as she eyed Simon's birthmark.

Simon stood up. "I think I hear some grasshopper sparrows."

"Oh, I've never seen them. Do you think we could find them?"

Lunch finished, they found the sparrows nearby and spent the rest of the day birding roads outside the park. They saw and heard a cactus wren making a racket with its harsh song, a green-tailed towhee, and numerous other birds. "We can come out tonight and look and listen for night birds," Simon said. "Or we could get up early in the morning around four o'clock and do that. We'll have a moonlit night. We don't have to have full dark."

Maggie voted for doing it after supper and leaving enough time for other recreation. So they ate supper at the motel and went back after dark. They played tapes of the calls and had answers from screech, barred, and horned owls (in that order, Simon told Maggie, because bigger owls eat the smaller). After that they enticed lesser nighthawks, poorwills, and paraques to call. The nighthawks and paraques flew in close for them to see.

That night, after lovemaking, they dropped off to sleep. Simon had one of his nightmares and his noise woke Maggie, who shook him awake and consoled him, holding him close and singing him back to sleep as she might have cajoled the child she had never had.

Awakened again by their early morning wake up call, they had breakfast and went out again to the state park and spent the morning birding. After a Tex-Mex lunch, they headed home, stopping for an early supper at Nate's in Jamaica Beach.

Maggie dropped Simon off at Trailer 10, still not wanting to believe that Simon was a killer or a rapist.

ℝ ℝ ℝ

Left alone with his thoughts, Simon decided the rapist must strike again, but his object could not be Shaper or Maggie. He could feel his suppressed anger rising. This time he would choose some woman not involved with Maggie or Patsy, his object being to throw the police off the trail.

He would pick a woman who lived alone and had no connection with Maggie, Patsy, or Birds & Floats. He looked in the papers for women recently widowed or divorced for prospects.

Chapter Twenty

Bob smelled the scent of jasmine as soon as he opened the door to the house. He went to their bedroom to change his clothes and found the smell of jasmine was even stronger there. When he had changed, he found he too smelled of jasmine. Wherever he went, there was the aroma, even in the kitchen, where it mingled with the kitichen odors. He relished the combination.

Apron on, Georgie was busy. Had he not known better, Bob would have sworn her to be a jasmine bush, the strength of the jasmine scent around her was so strong. He hugged her and kissed her and twisted his tongue in hers. "You must have something interesting in mind," he said, rimming her ear with his tongue.

"Indeed I do. It's our monthly anniversary. Fix us some drinks."

"What would you like? "

"In view of the occasion, let's try something new. I'll take a margarita."

As he poured the tequila and mixed the drinks, Bob told her he had come to the conclusion that the Frank murder and the serial rapist were indeed related somehow. "Patricia Shaper is the link. We have had her under protection, but the rapist slipped by our stakeout. She surprised him after his attack and chased him off with her shotgun—she thinks she wounded him."

"It's good for a woman to be handy with a shotgun. I think I'll start practicing."

"I reckon I'd better behave."

He pronounced Georgie's salmon dinner delicious as he downed the last of his second margarita. "What did you plan for dessert?"

"I've been thinking. We've tried so many things. It wasn't easy, but I have found something. I hope you enjoy what I'llI do for you. You can do something similar for me, but I don't have the right equipment for the full implementation of it."

"You certainly have my attention. Where do we begin?"

"In the shower, getting clean."

Later, after drying off, they set lotion on a table by their bed for easy use. "I'm going to give you what's called a trip around the world. So just lie back and enjoy the journey."

Later, she asked, "Did you enjoy the trip?" "

"It was a delightful." He kissed her. "I'll do my best now to pleasure you. He moved gently to please her. Afterwards, they both took another shower before mixing new drinks. Overcome by jasmine scent by then, they turned to other adventures of love as they whispered endearments and how pleasant sex without rape could be.

"Why would anyone want to rape?" Georgina asked.

"Well, some people might deem your marriage proposal to me a rape, but I found it very enjoyable. My guess is that something happened to the rapist in childhood that pro-grammed him up to anti-social actions."

⁋ ⁋ ⁋

For a month Simon declined many of the invitations he received from Maggie, limiting himself to one evening dinner and one morning of birding a week. He told Maggie he was searching for a job he would enjoy, one that wouldn't occupy too much of his time.

Peering through the papers, he eventually found several prospects for the rapist: two divorcees and two widows, plenty to begin closer research. He wanted women living in situations that offered privacy and easy access. He ruled out any with large dogs, but he would consider a small dog or cat if he thought he could get rid of it with poison. The age of the prospect did not bother him, but he preferred a fairly young woman because she was less likely to die of fear during the rape. Beauty was not a major issue, but he required a location in Galveston, because he wanted the crime to be investigated by the Galveston police.

He chose a woman in her early forties whose older husband had died of an unexpected heart attack, leaving her in sole possession of a house in the conservation district. They had not been living there long before his death, so she should not have any close friends nearby, and his investigation revealed she had no dogs or cats. Her job as a substitute teacher at the elementary level must be to keep her occupied, Simon judged, rather than answering a need for money. As far as he could determine, she had not formed any close attachments with a male since her husband's death. So Ellie Endicott seemed like a prime victim.

He picked a night mid-week after a lengthy surveillance. She usually spent Wednesday nights at home alone. She had not installed a security system as far as he could determine, and he had found a window on the first floor that was unlocked. He had been in the house to map the rooms and had watched enough to know which bedroom she used.

The night he chose he made his usual preparations and drove after dark to the spot where he had decided to park, several streets away from her house. From there he walked the route he thought would be most deserted. It was a good choice. He saw nobody and slipped into his victim's back yard undetected. He waited until all the lights were out except in her bedroom before entering through his chosen window. He could see the light from her bedroom spilling into the hallway. He settled down to wait. After her bedroom light no longer flooded into the hall, about thirty minutes, he stepped silently to her bedroom doorway and peered in. A nightlight was on in her bathroom, shining a low light into the bedroom.

Ellie was sleeping on her right side, turned toward dim glow from the nightlight. Simon moved quickly to the bed, straddled her, pulled her over on her back and taped her mouth shut. He followed his usual routine to the letter, knife and all. Ellie pleaded with him not to hurt her by raising her hands in a prayerful manner. "If you remain quiet and do what I tell you without questions, I won't hurt you. You see this knife. I can kill you with it, but I have a pistol too. Do you understand?" She nodded.

"Okay." He took the tape off, and she remained quiet. The rape proceeded according to the ritual he had established except his victim showed little terror. Instead she met his thrust with greedy acceptance, upsetting his rhythm by holding him tight so that she could operate with the skill of an expert fellatrice. Taken aback, surprised, but overcome by the desire she instilled in him, he lost control and gave way in orgasm. Evidently delighted, he thought, she pushed him back as she savored him. Soon she was above him, straddling his remaining erection, sighing in what appeared to him to be delight as she took her pleasure with him.

"I haven't had any sex since my husband died. He was expert at pleasing my rape fantasy," she said as she tried to encourage him to further effort.

"Damn you, you've ruined the whole thing," he said as he tried to gather his thoughts. He was unable to resume his pattern. His desire for rape was quenched.

"Don't leave," Ellie pleaded. "Please. I haven't had any sex since my husband died." In the dim light, he could see her tears. "I won't report you to the police. Just do what you usually do."

Unaware he had been followed by Patricia Shaper, Simon sat down on the bedside, unsure of what to do, as Ellie pleaded. "If you don't go through with it, I will report you. Please, rape me as you planned."

As he listened, he was hardly able to believe what he was hearing.

When she continued sobbing, and tried to pet him, he decided he might as well humor her. Things weren't going according to plan. He was losing his desire to rape. Her tears completely disarmed him, as she encouraged him to please her with her oral expertise.

He would have been even more disturbed had he known he was being hunted by Patricia Shaper, who saw him when he entered the house and was watching and waiting when hours later he exited Ellie's house.

ⅎ   ⅎ   ⅎ

Several days passed before Simon called Maggie to see whether or not she'd like to come down to the beach for a morning's birding. "I know it's short notice, but the day is sunny and the breeze is very pleasant."

"I'd love to join you. Would you be willing to come here for lunch?"

"Sure, why don't I come by and pick you up and we'll go down to the beach at the state park. Wear your bathing suit underneath and we'll go in for a swim after birding, if that suits you?" Laughing at the pun, Maggie agreed.

"Great. I'll be ready when you get here."

They used Maggie's pass for the park and had a great morning watching birds on the beach and over on bayside. Egrets and herons were plentiful, white-tailed kites were active, and there were shorebirds on the beach feeding at the water's edge with a reddish egret, Galveston's city bird. Maggie had brought a beach towel, so when the time for swimming came, they just shucked their clothes on the towel and ran to the ocean. Soon they were out almost to her neck. "This was a great idea. You haven't spent much time with me these past few weeks," Maggie said.

"I would have preferred to spend more time with you, but I've been looking for a job. I haven't found any I wanted. I'll spend all of my time with you the next few days."

"Sounds great."

"You may tire of me."

"No, indeed," she said. She felt his hand as he reached under her top to massage her breasts.

⁞ ⁞ ⁞

Simon was quiet for a while as he continued massaging and kissing her, wrestling with the idea that he might be falling in love with Maggie despite all of his hatred of women. He kept remembering the comforting lady with the cookies and Ellie Endicott. He was still trying to make sense of what had happened at Ellie's. His main regret was that it might be too late for him and Maggie. He wasn't sure he could quit his rapes, but his last attempt had been completely foiled and had begun a relationship with a woman who was eager to be raped.

Even if Bruce and Jackson didn't catch up with him for the murders of Frank and Kanger, he was beginning to lose desire for rape. He had promised Ellie to make her the subject of simulated rape attempts. Otherwise she would report him to the police. He had to admit that he found his encounters with her very enjoyable. Simulated rape was proving a satisfactory substitute for the real thing. Ellie even enjoyed the cigarette burns though they hurt..

As he was trying to reconcile his hate-filled life with the positive feelings he had for Ellie and Maggie, he blurted out, "You know you're good for me, Maggie. You make me love life."

She laughed as she hugged him to her to feel him grow against her. "I want to have some proof of those feelings after lunch" They played in the Gulf for another half hour before Maggie began to feel hunger. "Let's go dry off in the sun a bit and then head to my place for some food."

The drying and the driving brought them to Maggie's a half an hour after one. Maggie pulled out some lasagna from the fridge and warmed it in her microwave. While it was warming, she made them rum colas, heavy on the side of the rum. Simon drank and ate with pleasure. "Maggie, besides all of your other good qualities, you are a great cook," he said, lifting his second drink to toast her.

Maggie blew him a kiss. "I'm flattered. Now it's time to reward the cook by having a shower with her."

On her bed, after the shower, Maggie asked, "Do you remember what you claimed earlier about the effect I have on you?"

"Yes, I recall what I said, and I meant it." Their lovemaking drifted into sleep wakened by Simon's screams, which woke Maggie, who shook him awake.

"What's wrong? You were screaming as if you were in pain."

"I can't remember exactly. It happens when I have nightmares about my mother. She drank too much, and she was sadistic when she drank. She tortured me with burning cigarettes and knives and cursed me as a useless lover as she forced me to give her cunnilingus."

Maggie kissed him and petted him until he calmed. "You must overcome your childhood terror." She kissed him again and cuddled him, holding him close. "Now, Baby, I'll show you what a happy boy you can be for Mama Maggie. After sex, he went back to sleep in her arms as she crooned a lullaby.

Next morning Simon woke first. "Wake up, Maggie, it's time for breakfast."

Simon's new awareness of his feelings for Maggie and Ellie caused him to worry that Bruce and Jackson would catch up with him and end this pleasant idyll that his life had become. He was aware, too, that he had to worry about whoever was making his life miserable with small attacks.

Ω Ω Ω

Idyllic for Maggie, Ellie, and Simon, but not for Patricia Shaper— she was becoming less and less a part of the happy life Maggie and Simon were living. Seething with anger at Simon for his rape and for stealing Maggie from her, Patsy was keeping track of him. She wanted revenge for his rape. She had promised her friend that she would not report Simon to the police, but she had not promised to be his friend.

She began by hurting him in small ways to irritate him. She let out the air in the tires of his car; she soaped the windows of his trailer and cut its wooden steps just enough so that they collapsed when he stood on them. Patsy learned of Simon's anger at these irritations from Maggie and did her best to conceal her satisfaction, happy in the knowledge that her victim was suffering. She had kept watch on him for weeks. When he set out on his rapes of Ellie Endicott, she had followed him and, unknown to him, observed his entrance but did not witness the startling reversal. She became mystified when he repeated his visits to Ellie. She determined to use them to exact her revenge.

She had promised Maggie to keep quiet about Simon's raping her, but she had not promised about any other rapes. She made an anonymous call to the Galveston police informing them that Simon Wulf had committed a rape at the home of Ellie Endicott. That done, she loaded her shotgun with birdshot and set out for Simon's trailer. With one barrel she peppered his trailer. When he stepped out to investigate, she peppered him with the other barrel, listened to his curses, and vanished into the darkness.

Chapter Twenty-one

aving met Emden's parents and passed muster, Steve had established himself as her steady, and they dated two or three times a week. Steve had accepted Emden's determination to keep her virginity for marriage, and he was trying to decide whether he was ready for connubial bliss. His partner Bob highly recommended it, but Steve was aware that Georgina had had to pop the question to Bob.

Steve knew he loved Emden, but he harbored a traditional notion that the man should be the family's breadwinner, and it was already obvious that Emden did not accept what she considered his archaic view of male/female roles. Her mother and father, especially her father, took Steve's side, but Emden remained adamant. If Steve wanted her, he had to adapt to her profession. She wanted children, but she did not intend to give up the career she'd worked so hard to achieve.

So they were at an impasse, but Emden's cleverness was not confined to encounters with corpses. She had been willing to play a waiting game, but she wasn't happy about such a long delay. She had the full support of Georgina Bruce, who told her that men often had to be led to the altar by extraordinary effort.

Georgina told Emden Steve wouldn't be able to hold out. He would be easy. When they were setting up for bridge after a spaghetti dinner, she told Emden to be firm. "Just stick to your game plan, Emden. He's so lovesick he won't last more than a few months, if that long. There's no reason for you to give up your career. Employers these days know they have to give maternity leave, if it comes to that."

As they played bridge, Emden asked about the wonderful scent she smelled. "What's that lovely aroma that fills your house. It makes me feel so blissful."

"Oh, I keep jasmine around the house; it has such a wonderful scent and such good effects," Georgina positively glowed as she discussed her appreciation of jasmine's wonderful qualities.

Emden sniffed the air again. "Its scent certainly is pleasant. It seems to affect the libido?"

"There's evidence that it does. Bob and I can vouch for that."

Like Georgina, Emden had kept up an intense interest in what Georgina still considered her case. Emden asked if the detectives had thought of using facial recognition to catch Mackensie Craft, "If he's the serial rapist, he must still be here in Galveston. If he sold his old car and bought a new one with a false name, you might be able to check Mackensie Craft's photo and compare it with any suspect you come across. You could get comparable photos from the DMV unless the suspect doesn't drive a car. You can send the pictures off to the FBI to use for their facial recognition analysis."

"We hadn't thought of that," Bob admitted. "We need something to help narrow the field of suspects. enough so that we can get a warrant. The rape of Patricia Shaper leads us to think the rapist may have an assumed a very clever disguise."

Steve looked at Emden with a funny expression. "You're one smart cookie," he exclaimed.

Bob saw what he called Georgie's puckish look and waited for her to make a shrewd observation. "Perhaps now that you've figured out Emden's very bright, you might want to consider her guidance in other matters," she said as she trumped Steve's king.

Emden smiled at Steve and squeezed his hand. "It's used for investigative purposes only. The Face service is part of CJIS (Criminal Justice Information Services). They analyze the photos and give you an idea whether you're on the right track. Texas cooperates with the FBI on mug shots taken for drivers' licenses."

"Thanks,' Bob said as he slapped his thigh, "that gives us a great way to check on any male among Margaret Smith's acquaintances to see if one of her friends is Mackensie Craft in disguise.

The bridge lasted until ten. Then Emden told Steve it was time to bid their hosts farewell. "I have a heavy day tomorrow, Honey. We had a great time, Georgina."

"I've fixed up some jasmine for you," Georgina said as she handed jasmine branches wrapped in wet newspaper and plastic to Emden before they departed. "Put these in water."

ℂ ℂ ℂ

As they drove toward her office, Emden asked Steve to go to the beach so that they could see the moonlight on the water.

"I thought you have a busy day tomorrow"

"I do, but I'm in a romantic mood. Maybe it's the jasmine scent from the cuttings Georgina gave me."

Steve drove to the east end of the Seawall and parked facing the ship channel. "Great, that's beautiful view," Emden said as she reached up to kiss Steve, entwining their tongues. Soon he broke away.

"That feels so good," she said as he began kissing her breasts.

"I enjoy it too, but I'd like to kiss more of you."

"There's a simple solution," Emden said.

Steve had been thinking about the solution she had already mentioned, marriage—a topic on his mind for weeks. He thought he ought to be the breadwinner of the family, but Emden had made clear her determination to remain working.

"I'm not asking you to stop being a policeman, am I?" she asked. Remembering the intense enjoyment she gave him, Steve still felt full of desire. He wanted all of Emden, but he still hesitated meeting her demand.

"No."

"Then it's not fair to ask me to give up what I enjoy doing." she said. as she unzipped his pants. "Steve, I love you, but I don't want to wait forever. Times have changed." She pulled on him enough to produce pain. "Will you marry me?"

"Ouch! Let go, Let go. That hurts. Set the date"

She twisted. "You won't back out?

"No, no .... let go. It hurts; I love you. Set the date." She didn't let go. She kissed him.

"In another month we'll be a married couple. Your apartment is big enough for two?"

"You know it is. We may need a larger one later. How do you feel about contraception?

"I know what the Church says, but I don't believe in having babies if you're not ready for them. So we'll plan for them."

⁊ ⁊ ⁊

The next day Bob and Steve began making plans to put Emden's suggestion into action. They installed camera equipment where it could photograph everyone who entered or left Margaret Smith's house, and they contacted the DMV and obtained permission to use Mackensie Craft's mug shot for comparison with any suspects that they needed to send to the FBI along for comparison with Craft's.

John Withers told them that an anonymous informant had reported a rape of a woman named Ellie Endicott two weeks earlier. "According to the informant's description, the rape followed the pattern used by the serial rapist. The anonymous caller identified the rapist as Simon Wulf.

"An interview with Mrs. Endicott proved unproductive," Withers said. "She insisted she had not been raped." Bob and Steve were puzzled.

After several weeks of photography, only one male had shown up at Margaret Smith's on a regular basis. He showed up many times, as apparently he was visiting there several days each week. Whenever he left her house, he was tailed, and they had soon learned that he was the Simon Wulf who rented trailer 10 at the Resthaven Trailer Park. As yet they did not have sufficient evidence to obtain a warrant to search his trailer, but they hoped the FBI analysis would provide sufficient reason to get one.

So John Withers submitted their request to the FBI with a plea that they make the analysis as soon as possible, since a case involving murders and a serial rapist was at issue. Then Bob and Steve waited for a reply.

When Steve used the time to ask Bob to be best man at his wedding, Bob expressed surprise that his colleague had acted so soon. "A few days ago you were still on the fence. What happened?"

"I think that playing bridge at your place had something to do with it."

Bob didn't understand what Steve meant. "You mean playing bridge forced the issue?"

Steve shook his head. "Not exactly. That jasmine aroma that saturated your house affected Emden. She asked me to marry her and insisted on an answer. She made it clear I'd never have her without marriage."

"I'll wait 'til tonight to tell Georgina. She didn't think you could last. She gave you six months at the most."

Steve grinned. "Yeah, I guess I was foolish to hold out as long as I did. I couldn't find a better mate than Emden. She's beautiful, she's smart, she's fun to be with, and she loves me in spite of my old-fashioned ideas. I decided I can adjust to a wife who makes more money than I do. She says I'd better get used to it, if I plan to remain a policeman."

Chapter Twenty-two

Though aware that he was under close surveillance by Patsy and the police, Simon Wulf was enjoying his newfound freedom from the urge to rape. Life with Maggie and Ellie had lessened his desire for rape to the point that he had little trouble resisting it. His performances at Ellie's, which he kept secret from Maggie, occupied much of his time, and many simulated rapes had satisfied whatever urge he still had for the real thing.

Whenever he sought good meals and days of bird watching, Maggie continued to cuddle him and sing him to sleep after sex. When he yelled out during a nightmare, she woke him and sang him back to sleep. His nightmares were occurring less and less. He hardly dreamed at all, and when he did, he awoke with happy feelings and Maggie in his arms, but he sought her care less and less as Ellie became more and more demanding.

When Simon appeared in the kitchen one morning after his last nightmare, Maggie gave him a troubled look. "You had a nightmare last night, but it had a new twist to it. We don't have time to discuss it now, but you and I will have to have a talk this evening or sometime soon. Now we'll concentrate on having a great day of birding on Bolivar," she said. He kissed her and said he would let her decide when their talk should be.

The ferry ride to Bolivar Pennisula provided a pleasant time for birding and dolphin watching on the upper deck of the boat. A pair of sandwich terms circled over their heads moving back and forth and calling, and a frigatebird sailed silently over without moving a wing as it rode the air currents with masterful skill. At the Bolivar landing, early migrant white pelicans sat on the piers alongside of cormorants and brown pelicans. Simon even spotted a pair of early red-breasted mergansers swimming beside the ferry as it eased into its berth.

Their first stop was the marsh on Frenchtown Road, where they were lucky enough to actually see both clapper rails and sora rails as well as hear the whinny of the sora and the *kek-kek-kek* of the clappers. "I've never seen or heard a rail to know it before," Maggie said.

"They're secretive. It's a great beginning for the day," Simon said.

Blissfully unaware of Jake Brockwurst, the officer following them, Maggie watched flocks of birds Simon pointed out. He enjoyed the birds too, but also noted the car following them. He saw an officer confiscating trash they discarded and made sure that Maggie kept one trash bag and he kept another separate from hers.

Their day went well. From Frenchtown Road they went to Ft. Travis and found a number of shorebirds feeding in the short grass, then on to North Jetty, where they found hundreds of avocets and other shorebirds, as well as herons, egrets and spoonbills. From there they went to Bolivar Flats, Rollover Pass, and High Island, where they had a late lunch. Maggie had packed chicken salad sandwiches and apples, which they washed down with lemonade she had made. They agreed they'd had a tremendous day in the field and were happy they did not have to wait very long in line for a return ferry. Simon noted with satisfaction that the police car following them was not allowed on their ferry. At Maggie's, he took his trash and locked it in his car to burn when he got home.

For supper, Maggie cooked pork chops with the help of Simon. After dinner she brought up his nightmare again. "Besides the woman burning you with cigarettes, you said some things that led me to believe you were reliving a current rape."

Simon sat down at the kitchen table. For a few minutes he covered his face with his hands. "I'm the serial rapist they're looking for, Maggie, but I haven't raped for months. You've changed me. Now I've managed to conquer my urge to rape. It's linked to my hatred of my mother, but the love you've shown me has made it possible for me to overcome memories of her abuse." He didn't feel the need to reveal his relationship with Ellie Endicott.

Maggie patted him on the back. "You and I have been living a pleasant life together. You've avoided Patsy, and I've managed to keep my friendship with her, even though it's strained. She won't go to the police as long as you leave her alone. Our relationship is not what society approves, and if the police catch you, they'll bring an end to our idyllic existence."

Simon nodded. "There was a car following us the whole day we were birding on Bolivar."

Maggie shook her head. "I didn't know that. We may need to move elsewhere. I believe you are overcoming your urge to rape, but I don't see as much of you as I used to. Are you still looking for a job?"

"I've thought of going to another country, but they'd just follow us."

"Maybe there're countries where United States law can't follow us. I'll start searching for a place that doesn't have an extradition treaty with the United States. I think I've read about one. It's a good birding spot. It used to be called the New

Hebrides. Now it's Vanuatu. Let's do some research on what it's like. Don't mention it to Patsy, if you should see her."

⁞ ⁞ ⁞

Officer Brockwurst thought back to the day before, when he received his assignment to follow Simon Wulf wherever he went and pick up any trash he and his friends discarded. He had scratched his head. "Are you kidding me?"

Bob had laughed. "No way, Rookie. It's important. We suspect Simon Wulf is our serial rapist and a murderer to boot. We think he's Mackensie Craft hiding under an assumed identity. We need his fingerprints. So your assignment is no laughing matter."

Brockwurst had watched all day. He was sure he hadn't seen the birdwatchers get rid of anything he hadn't seen. To break the monotony, he'd started watching the birds they were looking at, but he didn't miss the trash deposit the couple made in Boy Scout Woods, after the two finished their picnic lunch. He couldn't see what Simon Wulf stuffed in his pockets. Brockwurst collected what he could and followed them back to Galveston, where another officer relieved him so that he could take his trash back to the station.

Holding the bag away from himself, Brockwurst delivered his collected trash to Bob and Steve, who were discussing their lack of success with trash they'd collected thus far. Bob thanked Brockwurst, dismissed him, and passed the bag on to John Withers, who had still failed to find any prints other than those of Margaret Smith.

When Withers had been through the rest of the day's trash, including Brockwurst's contribution, he still had found no second set of fingerprints. "This guy is thorough," he told Bob and Steve. "You may have to rely on the FBI."

163

"His thoroughness shows his fear of our finding his prints, so we have to keep trying. When the FBI report comes through we'll get a warrant and get those prints directly from the man." Bob said.

Steve shook his head. "If he doesn't think we're on to him. He might fly our jurisdiction."

Bob poured himself another cup of coffee. "Do you have any suggestions about other ways to get those prints?"

"Yes, I do," Steve said. "We can find him guilty of a minor charge of some kind, maybe a driving offense bad enough to bring him in and fingerprint him."

"Can you think of a charge?"

"What about suspicion of rape? Or reckless driving."

"We don't have enough evidence, and he's a careful driver."

"Well, let's keep a tail on him until we do. Maybe he'll slip up," Steve said. "If he's the serial rapist, he's bound to do it again. We just have to hang back and be patient. We don't want to do anything to put him wise without letting him out of our sight."

Bob nodded. "Brockwurst's been doing a good job. We'll ask him to continue the surveillance. You and I will spell him on the night duty. That's the most likely time ior our suspect to rape again."

Steve groaned and poured another cup of coffee. "Okay, I reckon we should since I suggested it, but it sure will cut down on our social life."

"We might save some woman from an unpleasant evening."

Steve had some other matters on his mind. He was looking ahead to his marriage to Emden. The date was set for late September, Emden wanted a church wedding to please herself as well as her parents. Once committed, Steve was quite willing to be married in a traditional ceremony.

Bob agreed to be Steve's best man, and he threw his friend a traditional bachelor's party. Emden asked Georgina to be her matron of honor. Emden looked gorgeous in her traditional white wedding gown, and her mother shed copious tears while her father gave her away at St. Pius Catholic Church in Pasadena. The reception had a traditional wedding cake with figures of a bride and groom to be cut and eaten. The small but noisy crowd wished the newlyweds well with rice and cans tied to a car with Just Married emblazoned on it. Steve had stashed his car at the Bruce place in Lafitte's, so they did not have to make the long drive to their mountain honeymoon in the decorated car.

Happy that the serial rapist had not interrupted the marriage,

the newlyweds flew to Tri-Cities Airport in Tennessee, rented a car and drove to the Breaks Interstate Park on the Kentucky-Virginia line. They bought some food in Bristol to take with them so that they wouldn't have to eat all of their meals in the Park restaurant. Emden made sure they had plenty to use in the kitchen facilities of their rooms. "We'll want to hike and use the swimming pool, but we'll be spending lots of time in our room," she told Steve.

He agreed. "I waited a long time to see all of you. I want to take a long look and kiss all of you for a change." He loaded their binoculars and bird and flower books in their luggage. They had been warned that the weather might have a quite cool fall chill, so they packed some warm clothes for hikes as well as bathing suits in case the weather became warm enough for them to use the pool.

As it turned out, the first week was rather cool, down to the mid- thirties at night, so they were quite happy spending almost all of their time in their rooms exploring each other's desires and sexual expertise and determining their respective culinary abilities. Emden had consulted Georgina on how to succeed in both the bedroom and the kitchen, and activities in both areas achieved happy conclusions. Steve was pleased there had been no news of more rapes in Galveston

Warm weather developed during the second week and the couple spent days hiking and, when a few very hot days arrived, time in the pool., reserving their nights for matters of love.

⁗ ⁗ ⁗

While the newlyweds were celebrating their union, Patricia Shaper was growing more and more frustrated that Simon had not received punishment for his rape of her. She continued taking her shotgun when she followed him, but now she loaded it with oo buckshot. The night before Emden and Steve returned, Patsy followed Simon as he dressed in his rapist garb and proceeded to Ellie Endicott's bedroom through a back window. Patsy was prepared. She looked for a position giving her a clear view of the window. She sat down on the root of an old oak in the back yard to wait, preparing herself for revenge.

Hours after he had entered, Simon was leaving. Patsy had dozed off and on for an hour but pulled herself awake before he came from the house and walked by her station behind the oak. As he headed toward the street, she aimed carefully and fired her Mossberg 930 shotgun. The first blast tore into Simon's midsection, followed by another that hit somewhat lower. He crumpled to the ground short of the hedge separating the yard from the street. As he moaned, Patsy slipped by him and disappeared through the hedge to the street.

When Ellie came out to investigate the shots, she found Simon's bleeding body. She looked around but saw nobody except Simon, lying bleeding on the ground. She checked and found that he was still alive and called 911 to report a wounded man who needed immediate medical assistance for a gunshot wound.

Ellie followed the van taking Simon to to UTMB, where he was put into intensive care as an anguished Ellie tried to quiz doctors about his situation.

ℂℂℂ

Back home in Galveston, aglow with happiness, Emden and Steve spent much time telling everyone about the beauty of the Appalachians, and their delightful honeymoon. Steve praised Emden's cooking in their apartment and the beauty of the fall woods. "You should take Georgina up there some-time," he told Bob. "The reds and yellows and varying shades in between were really beautiful. Or you could go earlier in the summer and go to the Highland Games at Grandfather Mountain. Buy a kilt and wear it."

The honeymoon over, the couple were tired but bubbling with happiness. Georgina invited them over for a salmon dinner. As she and Emden talked in the kitchen before dinner, Emden thanked Georgina for her advice. "I'm very happy with marriage. I'm glad I followed your advice and pushed Steve into marrying. He's a very tender lover and an enjoyable companion. Even on our hikes he sat me down on a fallen log now and then to rest."

Bob and Steve were pleased when, a day after Steve returned to work, they received the FBI analysis confirming their suspicions that Mackensie Craft and Simon Wulf could be the same person. Bob slapped Steve on the back after they read the report. "This should shorten the work," he said. "We can get a warrant to search his trailer. We'll bring him in for fingerprints whether we find anything or not."

So the search for Simon Wulf began. Bob and Steve looked at his trailer and at Margaret Smith's house but found him neither place. They obtained his fingerprints but were baffled. He seemed to have suddenly slipped away from Galveston.

Chapter Twenty-three

That night after her shooting Simon, Patsy had stolen through the hedge separating Ellie's yard from the street. Making her way to her car, she hid her shotgun in her trunk and drove away, satisfied she had wounded Simon so severely that he might be near death. She checked at the hospital the next day and learned that a man with a gunshot wound was in critical condition in intensive care. Feeling she had achieved her revenge, she called Maggie and suggested they go birding. "We could meet at Lafitte's and spend tomorrow morning watching for fall migrants, then have lunch at Nate's." Maggie accepted the invitation without hesitation, so Patsy assumed she hadn't heard about Simon's mishap.

The fall migrants provided enough excitement with water birds and woodland birds to keep the two of them busy for the entire morning at Lafitte's. "This seems like old times," Patsy said. "It's been almost a month since we've been birding together."

"Yes, I've missed our birding."

"I guess Simon's been keeping you busy."

"Not really, lately. He's been around less the last month. He claims he's looking for a job."

"He's been in Galveston almost half a year now. Do you think he's made other friends?"

"He hasn't mentioned any." Maggie raised her binoculars. "Look, there's a male redstart."

"How beautiful … breathtaking when they spread their red tail spots." Patsy agreed as she pointed out a yellow-breasted vireo perching in the sunshine. "I'm a little thirsty." She looked at her watch. "It's almost noon. I think it's time for lunch. Let's get to Nate's."

Maggie turned to go, and they were soon drinking beer at Nate's.

"I've been calling Simon for several days without getting an answer. He didn't tell me he was going out of town. I wonder what has happened to him," Maggie said, after taking several sips of her draft.

Patsy was quiet for a minute. "Well, I don't think I'm the best person to ask. I've been trying to avoid him for months," she finally said.

"I know, and I'm sorry I let him take up so much of my time. I've neglected you."

"If I were you, I'd ask the people in the trailers near his whether they've seen him lately. If they haven't, maybe you should check the hospital."

Patsy saw a worried expression on Maggie's face.

"Do you think something bad has happened? It's been over a week since I've heard from him," Maggie said.

Patsy leaned forward. "I'm not trying to alarm you. Maybe he's made some friend or friends you don't know about, but you won't be content until you find what's happened to him. Maybe the police arrested him. You could start there."

"I guess you're right. I'll go by and ask Detective Bruce on my way home."

Patsy couldn't help allowing herself a secret smirk. *He won't be doing much with you. Even if he lives, he won't be up to much birding or sex for a long time.*

⁍ ⁍ ⁍

Maggie stopped by the police station and asked for Detective Bruce. When he appeared, she greeted him with a question. "Do you know the whereabouts of Simon Wulf?"

"No, I don't. We were hoping you could tell us."

"I haven't seen him since last week. Patsy suggested I should look for him at the hospital. Have you tried there?"

"No, he slipped by our men who were following him several days ago, and we couldn't find him at his trailer or at your place. Maybe he has had an accident. We'll look for him at UTMB. They should notify us if he's been brought in for what appears to be a possible felony. If you see him or learn something about his whereabouts, please let us know."

Still worried, Maggie made her way to UTMB and asked if they had admitted a man named Simon Wulf in the last few days.

The woman at the entrance desk checked. "Yes, he was admitted two nights ago with serious gunshot wounds and has been in intensive care since then. "

"Have the police been notified?"

"Yes, they were notified when he was admitted, but he was a John Doe at that point. We didn't discover his identity until today. The information was passed on to the police as soon as we knew."

⁍ ⁍ ⁍

Elllie Endicott had stayed at UTMB for several hours after Simon was shot and put in Intensive Care. When the surgeons told her they thought the patient was going to live, she went home to bed. It was late in the afternoon when she woke. She called the hospital and learned John Doe was still in intensive care. Tired, she turned on the television and watched the evening news before eating a light supper of yogurt and going back to bed.

Next morning, she drove to the hospital to check on Simon. She introduced herself as Simon Wulf's fiancée and offered identify whether he was their John Doe, who was still in intensive care. "He's Simon Wulf, my fiancé," she told them after they let her see him.

"He is doing well and probably will be transferred to a room in a day or two. We appreciate your identifying him and giving us other personal information so that we can pass it on to the police. Whoever did this to him committed a felony. It's doubtful he can walk any time in the immediate future, if ever."

After offering to help identifying the John Doe, Ellie still waited, hoping for more information; she was there when Margaret Smith arrived. The woman manning the entrance desk pointed Ellie out for her. "That woman claims to be our John Doe's fiancéee. Maybe you know her."

Taken aback by this information, Maggie hesitated. "Obviously," she thought to herself, "Simon has made some friends he didn't tell me about."

After watching Ellie several minutes, Maggie walked over to her and introduced herself. "I'm a friend of Simon Wulf. That lady told me you are his fiancée."

"Yes, I told them that so I could get to see him. I'm sure the John Doe is Simon. His medical condition is improving. He was shot as he was leaving my house two nights ago."

"Did you know the police are looking for him? I expect they'll place a guard on him before too long."

"How do you know that?"

"They told me they were looking for him to arrest him for murder and rape. I'm involved because Simon and I are friends, I was surprised to learn he has a fiancée."

"Well, he'll be lucky to live to be tried for those crimes. Whoever wielded that shotgun came near killing him. The issue's still in doubt, but now they think he'll live."

Maggie noted the mention of a shotgun. She immediately thought of Patsy.

The women's conversation was interrupted by the entrance of Detective Robert Bruce and several uniformed officers, whom he sent to guard Simon Wulf, more to make sure nobody could finish killing him than to stop him from fleeing , Maggie guessed, as she had heard the doctors assure Bruce that Simon could not now possibly leave without considerable help.

Bob recognized Margaret Smith, but not Ellie Endicott. Maggie introduced him to Ellie. "She says she's Simon's fiancée."

Bob remembered the name. "Your name's familiar to me. Somebody reported that Simon raped you, but you told our investigators you weren't raped. Am I correct?"

"Yes."

"I think we'll need to interview you before Simon Wulf comes to trial for murder and rape as Mackensie Craft, so don't leave town without telling us."

Looking at Ellie, who had sat back down, her face drained—by surprise, Maggie surmised. "I guess you're as surprised to think of Simon as a killer as I am to find out he is your fiancé."

℘   ℘   ℘

Maggie called Patsy as soon as she reached home. "Could you come over for supper? I'll put on some pork chops and warm up some vegetables. I have a lot to discuss with you over wine."

"I'll be over as soon as I shower."

As they ate and drank, Maggie told Patsy about her meeting with Ellie Endicott. "She says she's Simon's fiancée."

Patsy laughed. "A love affair that began with a rape."

"But she told the police that he didn't rape her. Bob Bruce claimed that they investigated a call about rape at Endicott's place and she said she hadn't been raped."

Patsy gave way to loud laughter.

"What's so damn funny?"

"She must have enjoyed being raped and enlisted him to repeat performances."

"What makes you think that?"

"Because I've been following him for months, I'm the one who reported a rape at Endicott's. He's been visiting her that long."

"That's why you told me he might have made other friends?"

"Yes."

"Then you're the one who shot him?"

"It's a wonder he's still alive after all the buckshot I put in him."

"Then I'll make more rum colas. It's time for a celebration. Let's go to the kitchen. We'll have ice cream and cookies with our drinks."

As they sat drinking and eating, Maggie was still trying to get her head around the news. "The two-timing bastard deserved what he got. I'm sorry I didn't believe you when you told me about the birthmark."

"My anger took over. I was beginning to believe the police would never catch the son of a bitch. I just couldn't wait any longer."

Maggie and Patsy spent much of the night celebrating Simon's arrest and reviving their old relationship. Maggie could not blame Patsy for seeking revenge. After all, Patsy had had to survive two rapes by people she had trusted. Maggie took the lead in forgiveness. "If you can forgive me for brushing our relationship aside, I must forgive you for trying to kill Simon. If I'd known he was two-timing me, I might have been tempted to do it myself."

"I forgive you."

"It remains that you're guilty of attempted murder, and I'll be guilty of obstruction of justice and perjury if I give you an alibi. It would be dangerous for us to hang around after Simon's trial. I don't think we could hide ourselves as well as Simon did, and he might figure out that you shot him and I lied for you. He'd be sure to tell the police."

"Yes, but where can we go?"

"I think I know the perfect place."

Chapter Twenty-four

At their searches of Simon's trailer and Maggie's house, Bob and Steve had found brochures touting the pleasant life available in the Pacific nation of Vanuatu, which had declared itself a republic. Their chagrin increased when they looked into the nation of Vanuatu. Bob had cursed when he discovered Vanuatu does not have an extradition treaty with the United States. "There's no way we could have nabbed him if he had made it to Vanuatu," he told Steve. "He had caught on we were closing in."

Steve threw a Vanuatu brochure across the office. "We know why he bought airline tickets for Australia. It's a logical stopover on the way to Vanuatu."

Bob had griped to Georgina. "Damn it, we solved cases, but it was just luck we caught the killer and rapist." He did not find the amusement on her face comforting.

"Well, I'm sure Chief Henderson appreciates your solving the cases, and the Chamber of Commerce is glad there isn't a serial rapist to worry about anymore. They've told me so when I've sung your praises. Besides, you might never have caught the murderer without us women."

"Maybe Steve and I'll get a raise. I wonder if Smith knows her lover was raped by our rapist, who apparently was also her lover?"

Georgina grinned. "I imagine she knows. You shouldn't begrudge her a little fun. Maybe you were a switch-hitter too before I roped you." Bob shook his head and retreated into silence.

"Clearly," she continued after the quiet had become deafening, "from what you and Steve have told me, Shaper has been more than a casual friend of Margaret Smith, even though Smith may have kept Wulf's plans secret from Shaper."

Further investigation by Bob and Steve revealed Shaper's pregnancy had produced a child, and that Margaret Smith had been spending time at the hospital with Shaper and had once visited Simon Wulf, who was still recovering from wounds inflicted by a shotgun. Simon's other, more frequent visitor, had been Ellie Endicott.

℘ ℘ ℘

Still angry with Simon for neglecting her for Ellie, Margaret Smith had argued with herself about giving Patsy an alibi for the evening of the assault. Maggie had told Detectives Bruce and Jackson, "Patsy spent the evening with me. I'll be glad to testify she was with me when he was shot." She realized that she would be guilty of perjury if she repeated her statement under oath, and the idea of escape to Vanuatu became both inviting and necessary.

The police took Wulf's fingerprints in the hospital and put a guard at his door after they put him under arrest—for his protection to begin with and—as he improved, to make sure he didn't escape to the arms of Ellie Endicott.

℘ ℘ ℘

Months after Simon was tried and convicted, Bob learned that Margaret Smith had bought three tickets for Australia.

By that time the pair fleeing American justice had made a life for themselves as law-abiding citizens in Port Villa, the capital of the Pacific Republic of Vanuatu. They had set up a business they called Vanuatu Financial and Tourism Services, working with the Vanuatu Tourism Office. Maggie headed the financial arm and Patsy headed the tourism branch, but each helped the other. Patsy was especially helpful leading birding and eco-tour groups. She had become an expert in the flora and fauna of Vanuatu.

To those who inquired, Patsy and Margaret introduced themselves as Mother and Daughter. The couple lived together in a comfortable bungalow in one of the better residential sections of Port Villa with Patsy's daughter. Surrounded by the aromas of tropical flowers and the brilliance of colorful tropical birds, they both delighted in the beauty of the island's plant and animal life. They enjoyed the plentiful bounty of the local fish at mealtimes.

They had managed to re-crreate much of the life that had been available in Galveston, although now Margaret and Patsy had business interests to manage. They ran their businesses out of a front room they had converted to an office in their bungalow. They had an adjacent small bungalow with rooms they rented to tourists.

Relying heavily on the internet to advertise their business activities, which they had tied in to the Vanuatu government's official tourism efforts, the women confined their business efforts to two or three hours in afternoons between one and four. Mornings were devoted to birding and other recreations or, upon occasion, special arrangements for leading guided eco-tours of the island. Their home was filled with a scent from potted plants that reminded them of the jasmine scent in Maggie's Galveston house. Evenings included sipping margaritas or fruit-rum drinks on the back verandah, where they often took their evening meals beside their pool to begin their evening activities.

Patsy's attempted murder remained their secret. Maggie had completely approved her shooting of Simon. Maggie thought their past was truly behind them. After a year, Patsy's dreams of vengeance had become pleasant fantasies inhabited by Maggie's comforting care.

In trying to come up with advertising gimmicks, Maggie thought of a humorous way to make their company known in America. As they sat one evening after their meal of local fish, fruit and vegetables, drinking fruit juice mixed with rum, she proposed a new advertising plan. "I think we should have a smiling family picture of us put on a postcard advertising the beauties of Vanuatu—maybe our pictures imposed over several beautiful views of our adopted nation."

Patsy laughed. "Who should we put on our mailing list? It wouldn't cost much to make a great many and charge it off to advertisement."

Maggie put her hand on Patsy's arm. "I think we should send at least one to the Galveston police."

Patsy nodded. "I think we should send at least one or more to Birds & Floats. Their members would love Vanuatu."

That night, as they lay in bed, Patsy asked Maggie a delicate question. "You and I have become close friends. I owe this wonderful life to you. Would you like to try for a baby?"

"I wouldn't mind, but I'm not sure I can become pregnant anymore."

"Would you be willing to try?"

"Yes, it's a great idea. I'd be glad to try. We have a sperm donor. I would like to try Hank's that he and I put away. I've always wanted his baby, but I was afraid to raise a child alone."

‣ ‣ ‣

So, when Bob, Steve, Emden and Georgina each received a post-card from Vanuatu a year later, inviting them to Vanuatu, the smiling family portrait of Patricia, her daughter, and a pregnant Margaret Smith stood beside beautiful scenes of Vanuatu. These postcards provided a topic of conversation and much laughter at the Bruce and Jackson households in Galveston.

"It's a wonder they didn't include a picture of a little cur-lew on the postcard," Georgina said, as she helped Bob set up the card table.

Emden laughed. "I think we should take a trip to Vanuatu to visit the happy family. Maybe I'll send a letter to their company to inquire about the pleasures of Vanuatu and how much they would charge to arrange a trip for us."

Bob and Steve were less inclined to laughter and less eager to travel. "They sure put one over on us," Bob said. "Maybe it's all for the best."

Enjoying the fragrance of jasmine surrounding them, Georgina said, "You have to admit, we haven't heard of any murders or serial rapes on Vanuatu. Maybe those women have found happiness. *Amor vincit omnia.*"

The End